IN THUG LOVE WITH A CHI-TOWN MILLIONAIRE 2

J. DOMINIQUE

In Thug Love With A Chi-Town Millionaire 2

Copyright © 2022 by J. Dominique

All rights reserved.

Published in the United States of America.

Published by Cole Hart Signature, LLC.

Mailing List

To stay up to date on new releases, plus get information on contests, sneak peeks, and more,

Go To The Website Below...

www.colehartsignature.com

PREVIOUSLY.......
CA'MAHRI

I had a lot on my plate with work, school, and my blossoming relationship with Dinero, but I was managing to juggle it all surprisingly well. Despite our schedules conflicting a lot, we were still able to make time for each other, and most of the time he was encouraging me to do my work or helping me study. I'd never had that before outside of my family. I was used to niggas not thinking that school was as important as your hustle, because the future was limited to the next day, or week or month. Dinero was different, he was already asking me about my goals after school and what I wanted to do with my degree. That shit was sexy as hell, and only made me want to be under him even more, despite the shit Cash had done. I didn't want to believe that he was capable of the same things but if I was being honest, the thought was gnawing at the back of my mind, that he may have been too good to be true. It didn't help that Camille was now on a rampage and trying to shit on anything love or relationship related, just like she'd been before she met Cash.

It was one of the first days we'd all had off together and we decided to spend it with our parents since we barely were able to get together, but as soon as my mama pulled out the margaritas my daddy had disappeared. He didn't play that drinking with his little girls shit and he also knew the type of conversation that was going to happen once the liquor kicked in. Now we were sitting around the table working on our second drinks each and playing card games as we talked.

"I'm just sayin', you better keep an eye on that nigga, 'cause ain't no tellin' what he doin' over there with his live-ins," Camille pointed out with her face balled up, and Noelle nodded in agreement. Rolling my eyes, I took a sip of my drink and pulled a card from the deck, inspecting it briefly before setting it aside.

"Dinero doesn't have live-ins. He cleans up behind himself and when he can't he calls a cleaning company," I said dryly, and they both looked stumped for a second before she went to try again and was quickly cut off by my mama.

"Camille, stop it. Dinero seems to be good for your sister, and unless he shows otherwise then you need to be happy for them. You too, Noelle, with yo' cosigning ass." She looked between the two of them sternly.

"I'm just sayin', Ma, dang!"

"Well, just stop sayin' 'cause you're soundin' real bitter right about now." Camille's mouth dropped and I held back a chuckle. No doubt her situation with Cash was unusual as hell and I definitely felt bad about it, but I didn't want her trying to put doubts in my mind about Dinero because she was mad at Cash at the moment. Unlike all of the other men she'd dealt with, I saw that she was really opening up with Cash and probably loved his ass, which was why she still kept in touch with his family. She thought I didn't know that shit, but Keshia had a big mouth and had already let it slip.

"I am not bitter, Allani—"

"Oh, these drinks too strong up in here if they got you callin' me by my damn name, girl!" My mama lifted up out of her chair and lunged at her, and we all fell out laughing.

"I'm just playin', Ma!" Camille threw her hands up, not wanting any smoke with our mama.

"That's what I thought, lil' girl!"

I was still laughing when I saw that Dinero was calling me and instantly, my stomach started swarming with butterflies. The nigga had me gone already and I hadn't even got the dick yet, which was crazy as hell to me. I figured he was waiting on the right time, but eventually I was going to end up just taking it if he didn't make a move.

"Hey, baby," I cooed, and all eyes landed on me so I turned away from their nosy asses to give us a little privacy.

"Oh, I'm baby now?" he teased, using my words on me, and I could hear the smile in his voice.

"You got jokes, huh?"

"Naw, I'm just fuckin' with you, but you still chillin' with yo' people?" The question had me looking back at the table, and all of them were tuned into my conversation but were playing it off like they weren't.

"Yessss."

"Ohhhh, you a lil' tipsy, huh?" he chuckled, and I had to agree because I was. My mama was heavy handed with the tequila on the second round and I was definitely feeling it.

"Just a lil'."

"Well, it's still kinda early so hopefully you good by seven, 'cause I got some shit planned for you. You think you'll be good by then?"

"Yeah, that's like five hours away," I scoffed, already planning how I was going to get out of not having any more drinks.

"Still gotta get dressed and do yo' hair and all that girly shit, so I don't know if that's gone be a lot of time with how long you take to get ready." Now I was really curious because he'd never really been worried about how long I took getting ready. Dinero was always full of surprises, though, so there was really no telling what he had planned, but I was excited, nonetheless.

"I'll be ready, sir," I groaned playfully.

"Ayite, your dress and everything is already at your house. I'ma see you in a few." He hung up before I could question him about what he meant and suddenly, I wanted to cut the day short just so I could go and see.

"Ohh, this heffa bouta dip on us, y'all!" Noelle was the first to speak when I turned back around to them trying not to look so geeked.

"Really, Cam?"

"In a little bit. He's not comin' to get me 'til seven, so I can still sit for a while," I promised, making them grumble while my mama waved them off.

"Don't mind these lonely fools. Let that man spoil you, baby," she encouraged, patting my hand.

We spent the next couple of hours playing a few games and listening to music, and I quickly lost track of the time. When I finally looked up and realized it was going on six, I hopped up and told their asses goodbye. I would still need to shower and do my makeup before Dinero's punctual ass showed up. Speeding home, I made it in roughly fifteen minutes and hurried inside to find two bags from Saks on my bed, and it took everything in me to bypass them and head straight to the shower. I jumped in so quick that I didn't even wait until the water got warm, but I hurried to wash my body, before running a razor over my legs and squirting Palmer's oil all over my body. For sure it was going to have me soft as hell. Patting dry, I wrapped my towel around my body and sat down on the edge of my bed while I rubbed on my Olay lotion and sprayed some Gucci Guilty on my pressure points.

By the time I finished with that I only had about fifteen minutes left to get dressed. I took that time to look at what Dinero had bought for me so I'd know if I should go all out with my makeup, and damn if my baby hadn't showed the fuck out. The strapless Monique Lhuillier dress had to be the most expensive piece of clothing I'd ever held in my hands and felt extremely soft against my skin. It was covered in sequins and had a high split up the thigh that gave the dress a splash of feistiness. As soon as I saw it I immediately knew how I was going to wear my hair and my makeup.

I quickly did a light beat, with a smokey eye and nude glossy lip, before smoothing my hair up into a high bun, and added a small gold clamp to add to the look. I kept my jewelry simple with just pair of diamond studs and a dainty gold necklace, since the dress itself was covered in sequins. When I finished, I stood in my bedroom mirror looking at myself in appreciation. The open-toed red bottoms had me looking grown, grown, and I already knew this would be the night. They had me feeling so damn sexy that I considered leaving them on when I finally threw the pussy at Dinero. The thought had barely crossed my mind and I heard the door opening and closing behind him, suddenly making me nervous.

"Calm yo' ass down, bitch!" I chastised, taking a deep breath and heading out just as he reached the hallway.

We both paused, taking each other in lustfully. Dinero always gave upper-echelon vibes but in the black-on-black tailormade suit, with a silk tie and shirt underneath, he looked like a CEO. My CEO. Shuddering, I had to tell myself not to lure his fine ass in the room and say fuck whatever he had planned, especially with the way he was looking at me.

"Damn, baby." Licking his lips, he rubbed his hands together and pulled me in for a kiss. "Let's hurry up and get up outta here before I fuck around and cancel this shit." I simpered as he grabbed my hand and led me out of there, locking the door behind us. Outside there was an awaiting town car and the driver stood with the door open, waiting on us to get in.

"Ooooh, fancy," I teased as we climbed inside, and he just shrugged.

"Oh, this ain't shit, watch me work." He popped the cork on a *bottle of champagne and handed me a glass before pouring one for himself. Oh, he's definitely getting some pussy!*

I still didn't have a clue where we were going and was confused as hell when we pulled up to the airport, right on the tarmac next to the huge ass planes. I damn near choked once we stopped and the driver came to open the door again. Turning to Dinero with wide eyes, I found him chuckling.

"Gone 'head, baby, you good." He nodded, gesturing for me to take the man's hand and step out. He came out right behind me and shook the man's hand before wrapping his arm around me and walking me over to a smaller plane that had its stairs out and the staff standing there waiting.

"Nooo, Dinero!" I tried to pull away in complete disbelief. "No! Stop fuckin' playin' with me right now!"

"Girl, if you don't bring yo' ass on, we already got a long ride ahead of us." I had only been on a plane a handful of times and they were all overrun with loud babies and rude people. This was clearly going to be a different experience and I was pulling him along at this point. I took my time climbing the steps onto the aircraft as the flight attendants all greeted us and led us to the seating area. Everything was covered in a light cream color with mahogany trim and looked almost too expensive to touch. The fact that I didn't have to just sit in a specific seat had my indecisive ass looking around for a minute before choosing a window seat on the left side of the plane. Dinero took a seat beside me, and a short time later the pilot came and introduced himself before revealing that we were going to New York, making my eyes buck. I don't know why, but I hadn't been expecting that we were actually going somewhere aside from riding around the city or something before going to dinner. Dinero had yet to make me feel like I was beneath him for being excited about shit he was clearly used to, but I still felt the need to reign it in. So, I didn't immediately start bouncing around in my seat like I really wanted to and that had

him looking my way once the flight crew finished their instructions.

"You cool? I thought you wanted to see New York." He was trying to keep it in check, but I could hear the underlying concern in his voice.

"Of course! Thank you so much, baby, this gotta be the best night of my life and it ain't even started yet." I bit my lip and sighed, making his smile return.

"You deserve all this and then some, but it's only up from here." Cupping my face, he gave me a kiss that I instantly felt between my legs as the plane ascended.

I swear flying private was the type of luxury a bitch could get used to, and by the time we landed I didn't even want to get off. Once again, though, Dinero ushered me off to an awaiting car, and I rolled the windows down as we rode through the city so I could see everything, while he pointed out landmarks that he knew from his many times there. He'd kept the night's events to himself, so I didn't even know where we were going until we stopped in front of a building that said Observation Deck. My brows dipped as I looked back at him, unsure of what we were about to do, but I was hoping it involved food because I was starving.

"Maaaan, just trust yo' man, ayite," he drawled as the driver came around and opened the door, helping me out once again. When Dinero's feet landed on the pavement, he closed my hand in his and walked toward the entrance. I was so busy looking in his damn side profile, though, that I didn't even notice a dirty hand reaching out to me until she'd already grabbed my arm.

"Do you have any change?" My breath caught in my throat just from the sheer surprise, but I quickly calmed down seeing that it was a homeless lady. I wasn't the type that thought I was better than anybody and knew that one decision could knock you right down to rock bottom, so I instantly threw on a smile. It was sad because the girl didn't look very much older than me. Her hair was matted into *a sideways ponytail that was full of visible dirt, and her clothes were a few sizes too small and looked just as filthy, and she didn't even have on shoes. By now Dinero realized that I wasn't trying to move with him and turned to see why.*

"Babe, do you have some cash on you?" I looked at him with pleading eyes, and he instantly frowned, ready to turn right back into the man I'd met that very first day. The silence on his end had her head snapping in his direction so she could ask him directly, but as soon as she laid eyes on him she gasped and tilted her head to the side in recognition.

"D-Dinero?" I looked back and forth between the two, trying to figure out how in the world she would know him, and was confused at the expression on his face as he dropped my hand and stepped closer to her.

"What the hell...Tania?"

CHAPTER ONE
CA'MAHRI

I stood off to the side with my brows dipped in irritated confusion as Dinero grabbed Tania up in a hug that was way too intimate for my liking. The minute he'd said her name my ears perked up, because he'd mentioned her in passing before. Even though all he'd said was that they were high school sweethearts, something in his voice let me know he had serious feelings about her. As a woman, I knew that piece of information was something to keep in my mental rolodex, and I was glad I had.

Dinero was so focused on her that he didn't feel the heat radiating off of me, and that only irritated me more. I wasn't so self-absorbed that I couldn't understand how fucked up this situation was for him, but at the same time I also didn't like the way this shit was clearly about to play out. Being the type of man that solved problems, there was no doubt Dinero was going to try to fix this, especially if he felt like it was his fault, which I was sure he did. He was already asking her what happened to her, with a look on his face that showed his concern and underlying rage. They both seemed to forget I was even there as she rambled an incoherent explanation to him about a baby, her father, and school that left me even more confused and him looking like he was about to kill somebody.

After her tear-filled confession, she buried her face in his chest, bawling while he rubbed her back with a clenched jaw. Pulling his phone out, he placed a call to who I assumed was the driver, and his eyes finally landed on me.

"There's been a change of plans, bring the car back around *now*! And tell that nigga Jeff to get his staff ready 'cause we're heading back tonight!" he barked into the phone, but whatever the driver said back must have pissed him off even more because his eyes darkened before shooting toward the street. "I don't give a fuck! That nigga works for me, not the other way around!" Hanging up, he immediately dialed another number and began yelling again as soon as they answered.

Even though I was used to this side of Dinero, it still made me feel some type of way because he was doing it for someone else; his ex to be exact, and I didn't know how to feel about it. He finally hung up and what felt like a second later, the car was pulling back up. The driver got out and paused at the sight of us. Confusion flashed across his face, and I couldn't even blame him because I'd been there the whole time and was just as lost on the situation as he was.

"Don't just stand there, open the fuckin' door, man!" Dinero fussed, making him jump into action. Swiftly, he opened the door and Dinero wasted no time ushering Tania inside. When he realized I wasn't following, he stepped back out onto the curb and reached for me. "Come on, Cam."

"I'm good," I said dryly, pulling my phone out so I could look up flights. This nigga had barely looked my way since he realized who Tania was, and now he wanted me to get into a car with them. I could already see this shit going left and before it did I would just remove myself from the situation.

"You're good?" he asked in exasperation, and the way his voice dropped had my eyes lifting from my phone screen. Squinting, he stalked toward me with his head tilted like he might have heard me wrong. "The fuck you mean you're good?" By now he was hovering over me, and I almost got side-tracked by how good he looked when he was mad. A shudder ran down my spine, but I shook away the wave of lust.

"Exactly what I said." I frowned. "That's your ex, Tania, right?" Immediately, his face fell and he released a heavy sigh.

"Yeah."

"Okay, well, you seem like you got some shit you need to figure out with her. So, I'm just gonna remove myself from the equation until you do that," I told him with a shrug. It was obvious they had some unfinished business and on top of that, there was the matter of her being a whole addict that he had to address. There was no doubt that he was about to get swept right up into whatever she had going on, and I wasn't trying to be around for that shit. Unfazed by the evil glare he was giving me, I blinked up at him waiting for a response, even though my mind was made up. I was thankful that we hadn't taken it there in the time that we'd been fucking around, or else it would've been much harder to walk away.

"Remove yourself from the....? Maaaaan, I ain't got time for this shit! Get yo' ass in the car, Ca'Mahri," he growled like that was going to scare me or something, but I just rolled my eyes. Dinero may have been crazy when it came to niggas, but I knew he would never bring any harm to me no matter how stern he was trying to sound.

"No! I ain't goin' nowhere with yo—" He snatched my phone out of my hand, cutting me off in the middle of me talking, and I wanted to slap his ass. "Give me my shit back, Dinero!"

"Hell naw! Fuck I look like leavin' yo' ass all the way out

here and lettin' you fly back alone?" he fumed, moving closer into my personal space, and I folded my arms indignantly. I had no intentions on getting in the car with him and old girl, and he was crazy as hell if he thought that I was. Our night had already turned to shit and had me full of mixed emotions. There was no way I was going to make myself even more uncomfortable by riding anywhere with their asses.

Realizing that I wasn't about to go willingly, Dinero nodded and swiped a hand down his face before dropping my phone into his pocket. The last thing I expected him to do next was sweep me up off my feet like I weighed next to nothing and stride toward the car.

"What are you doin'? Put me down, nigga!" I fought pointlessly, pushing against his chest and kicking my feet, but his hold never loosened until we made it to the door, and he shoved me inside while the driver just stood there watching.

"Go drive, muhfucka!" he yelled, making the man scramble away, before sliding in next to me to stop any chance of escape. I was literally trapped between him and Tania, who was looking on with wide, fearful eyes. The car pulled off so damn fast that my back slammed against the seat as I glared Dinero's way. He was looking at me just as intensely, like I'd done something wrong when all I'd wanted to do was get from around him at the moment.

The entire ride was tense as hell, and coupled with the sour stench coming off of Tania, I was ready to jump out and run as soon as the car stopped. What I expected to be a long ass ride back to the plane ended up being only a few minutes, and I finally tore my eyes away from Dinero long enough to squint up at the building we parked in front of.

"Aye, what the fuck we stoppin' for?" He'd been so busy mugging me that he hadn't realized we'd stopped until the driver opened the door.

"Sorry, Mr. Banks, the pilot says he won't be able to fly you back tonight, but first thing in the morning—" The silent anger emanating from Dinero had the man swallowing his words and even I was afraid for his ass. I held my breath, waiting for him to explode, but surprisingly he just pinched the bridge of his nose and let out an exasperated sigh.

"Ayite, man, just grab the bags while I check us in."

"Hold up, bags? You tellin' me we not goin' back home right now?" I quizzed, feeling myself about to go off.

"Ca'Mahri, bruh," he groaned lowly before stepping out onto the curb while I continued my rant.

"No! You should've just let me book my flight, but nooo, you had to do shit your way and now look—"

"Ca'Mahri! Shut the fuck up and get yo' ass up in this hotel before I carry you in there like the big ass baby you actin' like!" My lip curled in irritation but after the way he'd tossed me in the car, I knew better than to doubt his crazy ass. Rolling my eyes, I climbed out and was immediately awed by the sight of the massive hotel with a bright red W on the front. I already knew it was another expensive ass place like the one we'd just left, but I couldn't even be excited about it due to the circumstances.

If anything, my mood only worsened as I walked inside and saw how truly opulent it was. I kept my face screwed up the entire time Dinero checked us in as we received funny looks from both the guests and staff. I was sure they were wondering what type of weird shit we had going on, but they were all smart enough not to say anything or look too hard out of fear of Dinero's wrath.

It wasn't long before he was motioning for me to come on and I did so grudgingly, figuring the faster I complied the faster I'd be able to get away from him. With a bellhop following behind us, we all boarded the elevator and rode up to the twentieth floor. Just like in the car the ride was extremely tense and filled with both me and Dinero's pissed-off energy.

"Can I have my phone now?" I asked with a raised brow and much attitude as we ascended.

"No," was the simple reply he gave without even lifting his head from out of his phone, and I rolled my eyes childishly. He really had me fucked up, but I wasn't going to make a scene, especially since Tania and the bellhop were already looking uncomfortable. I was sure that she probably felt like I was feeling some type of way about her, and to an extent I was, but I was fully aware that us running into her was purely by chance. I also understood that she needed some help, and since it was obvious Dinero was going to go out of his way to be the one to do so, I just didn't want to stick around for the inevitable. This shit was about to turn into a romantic comedy real fast with a blast from the past love trope that was sure to bring them together, and before it came down to him having to pick between the two of us I would remove myself from the situation. I damn sure wasn't trying to get my heart broken after I'd invested any more time and energy.

Ten minutes later I was locked away in the main bedroom of our suite while he dealt with Tania in the other room. I was sure that he thought keeping my phone would stop something, but little did he know, I had Camille's number stored away in my memory bank. As bad as I didn't want to hear an 'I told you so' at the moment, I wasted no time dialing her up on the hotel's phone. Just knowing what happened would definitely have her jumping into action, and I'd be on the next thing smoking back home, even if I did have to hear her mouth about it first.

CHAPTER TWO
CAMILLE

"There's nothing coming out of New York to Chicago tonight, boo, and I looked everywhere, even on Spirit," I told my sister with a groan and closed out of my Safari app. We'd been on the phone for a half hour while she informed me about what happened after Dinero came and picked her up. I couldn't lie, it sounded like something out of a fairytale up until his homeless ass ex had crashed the party. Of course, Ca'Mahri being much nicer than me hadn't went upside their heads and was now locked in her room unable to leave because he'd kidnapped her phone. "Shiiit, want me to meet y'all when you land tomorrow and beat her ass?" I shrugged, making her laugh even though I was dead ass serious.

"No, crazy ass girl!" she managed to get out.

"Then you want me to beat his ass? Since I ain't got a chance to fuck Cash up I might as well get the next best thing." I rolled my eyes over the various flowers and other gifts that Cash had been sending every day since I'd left his house, and scoffed irritably. Curiosity had gotten the best of me, so I'd opened a few, but I fully intended to send all that shit right back to his ass. I wasn't the type to let expensive things sway me when a nigga fucked up and regardless of my connection with Cash, I'd already let too much slide. That was really why I was so mad to begin with. Not only had I disregarded my list for his lying ass, but I'd also let myself have hope that he was it for me. The fact that he didn't immediately get rid of that bitch Maria, knowing they'd fucked, let me know his ass never took me seriously, though, and I hated that shit. I'd fucked around and let him and his son get in my heart, and now I was stuck in my feelings about it.

"First of all, we already got a case fuckin' around with Walt's baby mamas, the last thing we need is yo' ass gettin' into any more trouble. Besides, he really hasn't done anything wrong except take my damn phone." My sister sighed. Without me having to tell her, she already knew that the chances of Dinero and his ex falling back into a relationship were pretty high. Not only was he going to feel some type of way about her having fallen on hard times, but the intimate act of him basically nursing her back to health was sure to reignite old feelings. Despite the shit I'd talked about that nigga, I really wanted them to get it right, especially since me and his brother couldn't seem to. Shit, I was still hoping for the best when it came to them because if nobody else deserved love, Ca'Mahri did, but I also couldn't lie about the issues a nigga's first love could bring. Before I could respond a text came through from an unknown number, and I already knew it was Cash without having to read it. His ass thought he was slick constantly hitting me up from random numbers since his was blocked, but every time he popped up with a new one I blocked that shit too. A second later, the same number was calling and I quickly hit ignore while my sister continued to vent. Everything she was saying was going in one ear and out the other, though, because *he* was calling back. This time I let it ring for a little bit before sending him to voicemail again. It was obvious he wasn't taking no for an answer tonight and I low key wanted to know what the urgency was. Cash never called so many times in a row.

"Ca'Mahri, let me call you back, I'm bouta see something real quick." I cut off whatever she was saying and without waiting for her to agree, I accepted Cash's call. "What the fuck you blowin' my phone up for, nigga! You ain't got the hint to leave me alone yet!" I immediately went in, and just like the cocky nigga he'd always been, his ass laughed, completely unfazed by my outburst.

"Stop fuckin' playin' with me Camille—"

"Ain't nobody playin', I told you I'm done so why are you still callin' me? Call yo' freaky ass maid and leave me alone!" I sassed, growing even more heated just mentioning her weird ass.

"Oh, you done, huh?" I didn't miss the humor in his tone as he asked, and it had my frown deepening. No doubt Cash had plenty of women tell him that only to turn around and still fuck with him, but I refused to be another one of his dummies. I was far from any of the weak hoes he was used to despite what he thought.

"Yep, now stop—"

"If you done fuckin' with me, come out here and tell me that shit to my face," he interrupted, and my eyes damn near popped out my head. That was the last thing I was expecting him to say since he had yet to show his face in all this time. "Don't get quiet now, bring yo' tough ass on out here!" The confirmation that he was actually at my house briefly had me nervous. Talking shit on the phone was one thing, but standing in his face was something totally different.

I was already off the bed, stepping into my slippers, and

heading to the door by the time I found my voice to ask, "You're outside?" Butterflies fluttered in my belly as I held my breath and waited for him to tell me what I already knew.

"Yep, and I want you to keep that same savage energy when you step out here too." *Cocky bastard!* My nose instantly turned up at the challenge, and I snatched the door open without even checking the peephole.

"You so full of shit! Yo' ass ain't even out here!" I stepped out on the empty porch looking for him as he chuckled lowly in my ear. There was no sign of his lying ass, and I wanted to slap him even more. Grumbling obscenities, I ended the call and reentered my apartment, making sure to lock the door back, and damn near jumped out of my skin at the sight of Cash sitting comfortably on my couch.

"Nigga, what the fuck! How did you get in here?" I shrieked, holding my chest.

"I got my ways." He stood with a slick smirk and advanced toward me, letting his eyes linger on the tank top I was wearing as a nightgown. Immediately, I started backing away until I couldn't anymore, and his grin widened. "What was all that hot shit you were sayin' on the phone?"

I fought to control my breathing as he stood over me, leaving little to no space in between us. Not only was he looking fine as fuck with a fresh cut, but he smelled delicious. He cocked his head to the side, awaiting my answer, and I couldn't help focusing on his lips as I tried to remember the question. It seemed like his chest swelled even more knowing he had me stuck like that. "Right, that's what the fuck I thought," he taunted, grabbing me by the hips and pulling me against him. "You can talk all the shit you want, but I know you miss me and that pussy definitely miss a nigga. That's who I came to see anyway since you on bullshit. Matter fact, I don't even know what I'm talkin' to you for."

This crazy nigga had the most serious look on his face as he dismissed me and proceeded to kneel while simultaneously lifting the hem of my shirt. Instantly my clit thumped, ready to entertain his foolishness, but I wasn't having it.

"Nigga, if you don't get yo' psycho ass..." My words trailed off as I bucked, attempting to move away, only for him to grip the back of my thighs, stopping me.

"What I just say, with yo' hardheaded ass? This an A and B conversation so see yo' way out our shit." The fact that he even thought that made sense just further proved to me how bad he needed medication, so instead of arguing with him I leaned against the wall with my arms folded. Taking that as his cue to continue, he took his eyes off me and leaned in close enough that I could feel his lips grazing my lower ones. "You miss daddy, don't you? I'm already knowing just from how you leakin', wastin' all that sweet ass pussy juice in these panties. Let me taste some."

Despite the insanity that was taking place, I couldn't deny how wet the fabric of my panties were. I had to bite my lip just to keep from moaning at the freaky shit he was saying and the friction he was applying. I was still trying to be mad, but at this point I was anticipating the feel of his tongue.

Pushing my panties to the side, he ran a finger through my slick folds and we both released a moan. As mad as I wanted to be, I couldn't stop myself from thrusting my hips forward. My eyes were closed, but Cash made it a point to suck my juices off his finger loud enough for me to hear, before letting out a pleased grunt.

"You want me to suck on that pearl tongue, Camille?" His voice was suddenly huskier than usual and I knew he was expecting an answer. In order to keep some type of control, though, I kept my lips sealed but nodded, hoping his crazy ass would go ahead and bless me with his lips. "Nah, you gotta do better than that, baby. Tell me what you want me to do to you," he urged, spreading my lips apart so my clit stood exposed and flicking his tongue across it. By now I was so turned on I damn near came just from that alone.

"Baaaabyyyy!" I whined, hating how weak I was in this moment. Somehow, he'd come in and flipped the script on me to the point that I was the one begging. When they said the flesh was weak they hadn't lied, because I knew better than to let a nigga back in so easily, but that didn't stop me from snapping my eyes open and telling him exactly what he wanted to hear. "I want my pussy in your mouth."

I didn't miss the satisfied smirk he gave before burying his face in my wetness, but I was too busy grinding against his tongue to call him out.

Before I knew it I'd erupted twice, coating his face with my juices. *Nasty ass nigga!* I thought when he stood up and wiped his mouth then licked his hand clean. Inflamed, I didn't deny him when he pressed his lips to mine and fed me his tongue. We kissed passionately, as he wrapped his arm around my back, lifting me off the ground, and I instinctively wrapped my legs around him. The taste of my nectar had me sucking his tongue aggressively as he carried me to my bed.

I mentally chastised myself for letting things get this far, even as I allowed him to peel my soaked panties and tank top from my body, before removing his gun first and then his own clothes. That shit was just as sexy as the dirty things he was telling me he was about to do to me, and every reason I was thinking of to stop him was immediately forgotten when he entered me, swiftly filling me up. It felt like he'd knocked all thoughts out of my mind and all I could focus on was his voice in my ear.

"Damn Camille, baby, you feel so fuckin' good!" he groaned, biting into my neck as his body stilled. It only took him seconds to recover. After a couple of powerful thrusts he sat up, lifting both of my legs with him and pushing them down so they created a letter V. My toes were over my head and damn near touching the mattress, allowing him to go deeper to the point that I could feel him in my chest.

"Uhhh, Cash!"

"Cash what? You want me to stop?" he questioned, pausing to await an answer, even though I was sure he already knew I didn't.

"Nooo!" Once again I was the one begging, as I shook my head vigorously and attempted to wind my hips so he'd continue his assault.

"That's what I thought!" Smirking, he slammed back into me and the sensation had my back arching off of the mattress. "Fuuuuck, you wet as fuck! Play in that shit for me," he ordered, and my fingers quickly found my clit, rubbing counter clockwise aggressively to match the death strokes he was giving me.

"Mmmm, baaabyyy!" I bit my lip as my chest tightened and I felt my stomach quiver. His husky demands and steady strokes coupled with the pressure I was applying to my clit had me gushing as another orgasm took over my body. "I-I-I'm comin', Caaaash!"

"Fuck, me too!" he panted with his brows dipped in concentration as he sped up, and a second later he was shooting his seeds off inside me. That forced me right out of my sex-induced trance, ruining my post orgasmic bliss and pissing me off at the same time. As soon as he released my legs, I pushed his stupid ass away and tried to get up off the bed, but he grabbed my arm, yanking me right back. All that shit did was make me even madder, and I immediately started beating his ass!

CHAPTER THREE
CASH

I didn't know how I'd gone from nutting to wrestling with Camille's crazy ass, but I was seconds away from fucking her up. Instead of wrapping my hands around her throat like I wanted to, I managed to put her in a bear hug. She was still wiggling around and trying to fight even after I pinned her silly ass to the mattress. This was the last shit I expected to be doing after sucking on her pussy and delivering the grade-A dick I'd just given her. My gifts and constant groveling hadn't done the trick, so I just knew a good dicking down would bring her back, plus the fact that I'd put a bullet in that bitch Maria's head, but she hadn't even let me get that far before she started tweaking.

"Get yo' stupid ass off me and up out my house!" she said through clenched teeth, still bucking even though there was no way she was getting loose.

"Man, you better calm the fuck down! After the way I just fucked you I ain't goin' nowhere but the fuck to bed next to yo' crazy ass!"

She let out a maniacal laugh that had my forehead bunching, even more confused by how she was acting. "Ha! Nigga, I think the fuck not! You couldn't even drop off some dick right, over here nuttin' in me and shit like I wanna be stuck with yo' hoe ass for the next eighteen years! Take yo' community dick back home to yo' ugly ass maid!" she fumed, and it took everything in me not to kiss her.

"You mad about some nut, Camille? Yo' ass tweakin'!" Now it was my turn to laugh. "I been lettin' off up in you 'cause this is my pussy. Shit, yo' ass probably already pregnant right now!" I let her know, making her eyes balloon.

"You got me fucked up! Get off me!"

"I'ma let you up, but you better keep yo' muthafuckin' hands to yourself. I ain't playin' either, shorty. You can be as mad as you want, but if you hit me again I'm gone fuck you up," I warned, giving her a look so she knew how serious I was. Her ass was too heavy handed to be swinging on me. When she continued to give me the death stare without agreeing, I raised a brow.

"Urgggh, okay, Cash!" she grumbled, and I saw some of the fire leave her eyes so I finally let go of her wrists and stood. Instead of heeding my warning, though, her crazy ass hopped up like a ninja and slapped the dog shit out of me. "And you better hope I ain't pregnant either!"

Before I could even react she had sprinted into the bathroom, slamming the door behind her. I wanted to go kick that shit down and snatch her little ass up out of there, but that wasn't going to make the situation any better. Either my ass was maturing or I really fucked with Camille, because if it was any other bitch I would've been got the fuck on. Pissed, I quickly threw my clothes on, tucked my pistol in my back, and pulled my vibrating phone out of my pocket. Seeing the multiple missed calls from Dinero had my forehead bunching as I headed to the door. Last I'd checked his ass was going out of town with Ca'Mahri, and the only reason he could be blowing my shit up was if something had happened. I hurried to hit him back once I'd locked Camille's door and started walking to the alley where I'd parked.

"Yoooo!"

"Nigga, you ain't gone believe this shit," he sighed, and my ears instantly perked up. "Why the fuck we on our way inside the restaurant and fuckin' Tania walks up beggin' for change and shit. Shorty out here fucked up, and I know her pathetic ass daddy got somethin' to do with it!" The mention of Tania had me pausing just outside of my car, and my face twisted up in confusion.

"What the fuck?" I was still processing that he'd run into a bitch he hadn't seen in over ten years, and she was a fucking bum. What were the odds that she happened to be in New York while my brother was and just so happened to walk up on him and his girl? As suspicious as I was, I didn't think that shit was just a coincidence, and I hoped his softhearted ass didn't either.

"Exactly! Her ass looks strung the fuck out too," he added, sounding pissed off.

"I hope you left her hype ass where she was at or directed her to the closest rehab, nigga!" I spat, hitting the locks on my Range and climbing behind the wheel. His silence on the other end let me know he hadn't done either. Blowing out a frustrated breath, I hit the start button and glanced over at Camille's crib just in time to see her childish ass peeking out at me. I clicked the interior lights and waved, making her flip me off and snap the curtains closed. *Slow ass girl!*

"Maaaaan." Dinero's voice brought me back to the conversation. "I can't just leave her out here, nigga. This is fuckin' Tania we talkin' about." After pulling out of my parking spot, I looked at my phone with my face scrunched up like his ass could see me.

"The Tania who broke yo' simp ass heart, aborted yo' baby, and then dipped 'cause her daddy told her to? That's the one you capin' for?" I wasn't trying to bring up bad memories, but this nigga was really tweaking if he thought he should stick his neck out for that shiesty ass bitch. He was just now coming out of the slump she'd put him in, and he was trying to let her come back like everything was cool.

"I can't fault her for some shit that happened when we was kids, and she already told me that the abortion is the reason why she got hooked on drugs in the first place. What type of nigga would I be if I didn't help her out?"

"A smart one!" I scoffed, unfazed by any of the points he had made. To me that shit sounded like straight up game, and I wished he was in front of me so I could smack some sense into his ass. "Nigga, where Ca'Mahri at while you out here playin' captain save a hoe?"

"Uhhh, she locked herself in the room after I took her phone."

"Aw hell naw! Yo' ass trippin', bruh." I shook my head, already knowing he'd fucked up. His ass had shorty away from home, sharing space with his ex, and he'd taken her phone away. I wasn't trying to be selfish, but I immediately thought of how him fucking up would affect my shit with Camille. Shorty was already pissed at me, and the shit his ass had going on would no doubt make it harder for me to get back in good, especially after what had just happened.

I spent the entire drive home trying to get his simple ass to see how stupid he was moving, but when I pulled into our gate and saw my baby mama on my porch, I hung up without warning. Apparently it was "dirty ass ex day" and my baby mama had to make her appearance or the day wouldn't have

18   J. DOMINIQUE

been complete. Little did she know, she was about to get removed with the quickness, especially after the way she'd abandoned Kash. There wasn't shit for her here.

"Get yo' ass off my porch, bro," I ordered, walking right past her. I ignored the lust-filled look she gave before she realized what I'd said.

"Tuh! You sound stupid! I ain't goin' nowhere without Kash!" The look of seriousness on her face had me cracking up as I unlocked my door.

"Yo' V, gone somewhere talkin' crazy. You know damn well my mans ain't goin nowhere with yo' flaky ass!" I thought Camille was crazy, but my baby mama had her beat when it came to that psycho shit. Unlike my girl, though, Vernique didn't mean shit to me and I gave zero fucks about tossing her ass off my shit the way Uncle Phil did Jazz.

"You can't keep me away from him! I'm his mama—"

"Were you his mama when you dipped out to go on vacation? Or when you brought yo' monkey ass back and didn't even come see him?" I cut her off, jumping in her face. Just like I expected, her ass didn't have a single rebuttal, but how could she argue knowing she did the shit. She opened and closed her mouth trying to come up with an excuse, and I pinched her lips together so she'd stop looking like a fish out of water. "Get yo' dumb ass off my porch before I do me and Kash a favor and put you out yo' misery!"

I removed my fingers and muffed her, making her stumble backward before I turned my back on her. As bad as she thought she was, she waited until she was a distance away before trying to curse me out. I wasn't worried about any of the shit she was saying though. Her voice began to fade and I realized she was taking her ass up the road to my parents' house to dry snitch. Thankfully, they had taken Kash to The Dells for the weekend, so I wouldn't have to hear my mama's mouth about it tonight. Hearing her fuss was the last thing I was trying to deal with after dealing with Camille's crazy ass and Dinero's drama. I made a mental note to change the code on the gate and let the maids know not to let her in anymore, before heading to the shower to wash Camille's scent off of me so I could take my ass to bed.

I woke up with the intention of chilling in the house all day since Kash wasn't due back for another day or so, but after handling my hygiene and checking the fridge, I realized my shit was empty as hell. With Maria gone, I didn't have anybody going shopping for me every week anymore and my bare kitchen proved as much. I tried for a good five minutes to sign up for one of those shopping apps where somebody went to the store for you and dropped the shit off to you, but quickly got frustrated with having to put all my information in. Plus, I didn't like the thought of some random motherfucker coming to my crib. I didn't give a fuck about all the ways they claimed to be professional, all that shit went out the window when a bag was involved.

After throwing on a pair of gray joggers, a black Nike t-shirt, and my OG Stage Haze Jordan 1's, I tossed a Bull's hat on and was ready to go. I used my number-changing app to call Camille and see if she wanted to come with me, but as soon as she heard my voice her baldheaded ass hung up. She was clearly still pissed about the night before, so I was gone give her a little more time to cool off and try again.

I pulled up to Walmart and instantly screwed up my face at how many people were there at eight in the morning. That shit had me hesitating to go inside, but I was already there and hungry as hell, so I climbed out and grabbed one of the carts that somebody had left in the parking spot next to me. My rumbling stomach had me headed straight to the produce section, tossing a couple bags of grapes in my cart, one to snack on and the other for the house. I walked around the store eating and tossing all types of shit in my cart that I knew I didn't need but had a taste for since the grapes weren't doing shit for me. Turning down the frozen food aisle, I ran straight into another cart and immediately grew irritated. I prepared myself to curse whoever it was out, but my words got caught in my throat when I saw a little girl that couldn't have been older than eight standing on the other end.

"Danielle! See, this is why I don't be lettin' yo' lil' bad ass drive! I'm so sorry, sir, my niece needs her license revok—well damn." A fine ass redbone popped up out of nowhere and damn near fucked me with her eyes. She definitely looked like an Instagram baddie in the tight, rainbow-colored dress she had on that had her curves on full display. Compared to the other women I'd passed either wearing pajamas, bonnets, or both, she was fuckable, but Camille instantly crossed my mind. Just as fast as I thought of her, I shook the guilt off. She wasn't fucking with me anyway, so it wouldn't hurt to have a bitch in my back pocket just in case she kept playing me to the left.

"Give me yo' number and all will be forgiven." I shrugged with a grin, and she immediately flashed me all thirty-two of the teeth in her mouth, letting me know I had her. She wasn't Camille, but she was definitely a close second and something to do to take my mind off of her. Thirty minutes later I was leaving the store with my groceries and her number, with plans to hit her up in the near future.

CHAPTER FOUR
DINERO

I carried me and Tania's bags into my crib and dropped them by the door as she shuffled in behind me, taking in the massive foyer. After showering and washing her hair she looked a lot better, but the loose fit of the leggings and t-shirt she wore was a dead giveaway that something was wrong. We'd stayed up half the night as she ran down how after the abortion she'd gone away to school, only to be haunted by the way she'd left things. Drug use happened to be more prominent amongst students than anybody knew and her roommate had quickly turned her on to popping Xanax as a means to escape. Within two years those were no longer doing the trick and she found herself moving up the ladder to harder drugs. With her grades suffering, she lost her scholarship and that's when her pops found out, but instead of helping, he was worried about what the congregation would think of her drug problem. In fear that she would ruin what he'd worked so hard for, he sent her to live with his sister who was unable to control her either. She ended up in New York trusting the wrong bitches, and got stranded because her family refused to send for her. I was still reeling from the story she'd told me and in complete disbelief that this was what her life had come to.

I was used to the girl that was fine as hell and popular but down to earth and smart at the same time. To see her in her current state fucked me up, and knowing that I was partly to blame only made it worse. All this time my ass thought she'd let her pops marry her off to some square ass nigga and she was out there living life, but that was far from the case, and it had me ready to put a bullet in his fucking head for taking her away from me only to discard her like she wasn't shit. After finding out what she'd been through, I couldn't just walk away like everybody else had. I owed it to her and our unborn to look out for her, and that's what I was going to do despite what Cash was talking about.

"Hellloooo, earth to Dinero," she said, snapping me out of my thoughts, and the corner of my lips turned up hearing her say that old shit.

"I know damn well you not still saying that lame ass shit." I chuckled, running a hand over my waves. Her eyes lit up and color flushed her cheeks.

"Kiss my ass, Dinero!"

"I see you still can't cuss worth a damn either, huh?" It was good seeing her smiling and laughing despite everything, and I was happy to be the one bringing that out of her.

"Anyway," she dragged, rolling her eyes. "Back to my question. Do you really live here all by yourself? This is a whole lot of house for a bachelor." Nodding sheepishly, I scratched the back of my neck and looked around at my shit. I could admit that it was massive as fuck for just me alone, but typically I was barely there so I never really thought about it.

"Yeeeeaah, but during the week and shit I usually stay at my apartment downtown. I'm barely ever here."

"I'm surprised your girlfriend hasn't tried to move in, I know I would've." She giggled, and the mention of Ca'Mahri had my body tensing.

"We were getting there..." My words trailed off as I thought about the look on shorty's face a little while ago when we separated. As soon as the plane landed she collected her things and was setting up an Uber, completely disregarding the car I had for us. We'd barely had any time to talk because I couldn't leave Tania alone, and I didn't want to have the conversation in front of her. She'd already witnessed Ca'Mahri acting a fool from the restaurant to the hotel, and as bad as I wanted to assure her that it wasn't like that with Tania, I wanted to do it in private.

I planned to go check in on her as soon as I got Tania situated and had somebody come sit with her. I'd done everything I could to curb her cravings over the last few hours, but I knew eventually she'd be going through withdrawals that would have her fucked up.

"Oh." A sad look crossed her face and I instantly felt bad. I didn't want her feeling like she was the reason shit took a turn with me and Ca'Mahri.

"We good, T.... How 'bout a tour?" I quickly changed the subject and she seemed relieved, giving me a vigorous nod of approval. After showing her around and hooking us up with a couple grilled cheese sandwiches, I left her in the care of Bruno, one of our security guys. As fucked up as it was, I slipped her a couple sleeping pills so she wouldn't be too much trouble for him, but I didn't plan on being gone long anyway.

I pulled up to Ca'Mahri's crib and took a minute to figure out what I was going to say, but wasn't shit coming to mind. On one hand, I felt like she didn't have a reason to trip because I was just trying to help out an old friend, but on the other hand, I couldn't deny that seeing Tania after all this time had me feeling...something. Given the circumstances, that something could've been strongly fueled by guilt, it was just too early to tell. As selfish as it was, I wanted Ca'Mahri in my life while I figured that shit out, and I wasn't trying to take no for an answer.

Sighing, I finally climbed out and walked the short distance to her door, throwing a head nod at the few niggas that spoke. I realized after I knocked that there was a chance she wasn't there, but just as I went to call and see, she swung the door open with her face balled up.

She'd changed out of the t-shirt and sweats she'd worn for our flight and was filling the fuck out of a Savage Fenty sports bra and biker short combo. Unable to speak right away, I swallowed the lump in my throat as I took her in. Even dressed down and with her face free of makeup Ca'Mahri was gorgeous, and I had to resist the urge to kiss her pouty lips.

"Dinero," she said dryly, folding her arms over her chest as she blocked me from entering. I wasn't expecting her to welcome me with open arms after everything that had gone down, but I also didn't appreciate her attitude. She was letting her assumptions cause a rift between us, without any proof besides me and Tania's history. It had been so long since I'd dealt with a woman in this capacity that I'd forgotten how quick they were to make up scenarios in their mind, but Ca'Mahri was quickly reminding me.

Shaking my head, I chuckled bitterly and swallowed my pride to ask, "Can I come in?" Instead of responding verbally, she merely stepped aside. As soon as I was standing in the living room, I looked around like I'd magically find the right words somewhere around the tiny space. The TV was on, playing Jazmine Sullivan's latest album, and between that and the smell of Pine Sol I could tell that she had been cleaning when I arrived. For some reason, I liked that instead of going out and doing something crazy, she'd elected to cleanse her space, and I nodded my approval.

"Okay, so can we make this quick? 'Cause I was kinda in the middle of something." Frowning, I tried not to let her dismissive tone faze me, as I took a seat on her couch.

"Look, I didn't come over here to argue, I—"

"So what did you come for? Because as far as I'm concerned we settled everything last night. I got too much goin' on to be worrying about whatever it is you may be doin' with your ex. Thankfully, things didn't go too far and we can both walk away with a clean slate. No love lost." She shrugged, and I couldn't stop myself from laughing, instantly making her face ball up.

"How long it take you to come up with that lil' speech? I hope it wasn't too long, 'cause you really wasted yo' muhfuckin' time." I stood and closed the distance between us before she could think of a comeback. "Y'all women stay assuming shit instead of just asking what you want to know. Yes, shit ended fucked up between me and Tania, but my only interest is helping her get better and get on her feet. The last thing I'm tryna do is mess up what me and you got going on, not when I've worked so hard to get us here." My tone dropped as I stroked her face, looking right in her eyes so she knew I was serious. She sighed heavily and tried to remove herself from my space but I held her to me, not willing to let her go.

"Dinero, I'm really not tryna get hurt, especially by you. I just—I don't think I would be able to bounce back from that shit." I could already see her eyes beginning to mist, and I rained down kisses on her face. Tears eventually spilled over, and I kissed them away gently.

"I swear on my soul I'm not out to fuck you over, baby. Just give me a chance to love you."

Our lips found each other, and after a couple quick pecks I sucked her bottom lip into my mouth, causing her to moan lowly. Slipping my tongue into her mouth, I lifted her in my arms and carried her to her bedroom as my dick strained to be let free. Just thinking about how Ca'Mahri's honey-coated walls would feel had me on the verge of nutting like I was a virgin or something.

As soon as I placed her on her feet she broke our kiss and quickly pulled my shirt off before trailing kisses down my chest and stomach, while simultaneously reaching inside my shorts and gripping my dick in her small hand. We locked eyes as she slowly made my shit disappear in her mouth and down her throat with a moan. I allowed her to do her shit until I couldn't take it anymore.

"Fuck, Ca'Mahri!" I cursed, snatching her up by the hair so I could shove my tongue in her mouth. Within seconds we were both naked, and I licked my lips, anticipating the taste of her juices as I sat down on the bed and slid to the top, pulling her along with me. "Sit that pussy on my face, shorty."

Biting her lip, she prepared to do as I'd said, but at the last minute she flipped around so that we were in the sixty-nine position. I separated her lips with my tongue and latched on to her clit, sucking it softly until she cooed and arched her back. Stuck, she couldn't do shit but squeeze my dick and grind her pussy into my face.

"Oooh, don't stop! Don't—right there! Oooh, I'm coooom-mminn'!" Her body rocked with an orgasm and I had to wrap my arm tighter around her waist to keep her ass still. I lapped up every bit of her juices I could before slurping at her nub again, making her come again before slapping her on the ass.

"You done?" I teased, running a finger through her slit once she'd slumped completely over, breathing heavily. The tongue had her looking almost comatose and I couldn't help gloating. It took her a second, but she looked back at me with a smirk and lifted onto her arms. Still facing away from me, she planted her feet and slowly eased down, choking the shit out my dick until I was completely submerged in her ocean.

I bit my lip to keep from moaning out like a bitch at the feel of her silky walls enveloping me, and she still hadn't even started moving yet. She braced herself against my legs, raising all the way up and then slamming down.

"Shit, baby," I grunted, mesmerized by the way her ass jiggled as she bounced up and down, occasionally doing some type of slow wind that had my toes curling. The room quickly filled with the sounds of her wet ass pussy and the loud moans she was releasing.

"Mmmmh, Dinero, shit that feels so good, baby!"

"You like that?" I taunted. With a cheek in each hand, I let my thumb slip in her ass, making her go wild, squirting all over.

"Yessss! Oh my god, oh my god, I'm comin' again!" Sitting up, I wrapped an arm around her and turned her over so that she was on all fours.

"Arch that back," I panted, and she pressed her face into the mattress and lifted her ass high in the air. I took a second to tongue kiss her clit one more time before slamming into her. Switching positions didn't do shit but buy me a few more pumps before I felt my nut rising again. "Fuuuck, you wet as hell!"

"Ummm, Dinero," she whined into the mattress when I smacked her ass.

"Shit, you ready to catch this nut, bae?" Her mouth hung open and she moaned her answer and began to match my strokes, bringing me closer to the edge. Pulling out of her, I held my dick and Ca'Mahri quickly spun around, wrapping her lips around the head just in time for me to coat her mouth with my seeds. A nigga was jerking and cracking my toes as she swallowed every drop and licked her lips greedily. "Damn girl, you tryna get a ring?" I gasped, falling on the bed beside her, and we both laughed, even though I was only partially joking. Low key, Ca'Mahri had the type of pussy that I'd kill a nigga over and wouldn't feel no type of way about it.

"Maybe." She cuddled up next to me giggling, and I wrapped my arm around her, noting how good she felt laid up against me.

"Word? The way you just drained a nigga, I'm ready to take yo' ass to Vegas right now!"

"Aht, aht! If you gone put a ring on it then I want a big fancy wedding. You ain't bouta shortchange me, nigga." Nodding, I traced a hand along her side.

"When that day comes, I definitely got you," I promised, meaning every word, and surprising myself. I'd gone from not knowing what to say, to promising not to hurt her and damn near proposing. Shit was crazy and I could only hope I was able to keep my word with Tania's reappearance, but I was definitely going to try my best.

CHAPTER FIVE
CA'MAHRI

It had been a couple weeks since me and Dinero made things truly official and even though I talked to him every day and had even seen him at least twice since then, I was still feeling some type of way. Mostly because he was even busier than before. Between monitoring Tania and helping to run the family businesses he was constantly running around. Thankfully, I was just as busy since I'd started working at Rush and had begun my nursing classes, but that didn't stop me from missing him.

I checked my phone for what seemed like the hundredth time and fought down the irritation I felt brewing. I'd texted him hours ago asking if he wanted to grab some food after my shift and he had yet to answer. Sucking my teeth, I set my phone face down and finished the charting I was doing.

"Girl, what's yo' problem?" Noelle, who was sitting next to me, asked with a raised brow. Knowing that she felt the same way about Dinero's situation that Camille did, I wasn't about to play myself and tell her shit.

"Nothin' girl, I'm just ready to go." I rolled my eyes, and she gave me a look like she knew my ass was lying.

"Mmhmm. Well, you wanna go to The Punchbowl with me and Camille so I can beat both y'all hoes in bowling?" She smirked and did a little dance in her seat.

"Girl boom, you be havin' the nerve to talk the most shit knowing you're the worst player. I'll definitely go though. I ain't got shit else to do, might as well go beat yo' non-bowling ass and get drunk while I'm at it."

"Yeah, ayite hoe!" Her ignorant ass waved me off just as someone approached the desk to be checked in. She instantly put on her professional voice like she hadn't just been cursing like a sailor. Pursing my lips, I got back to my charting while she handled the patient. They must have scheduled everybody back to back because right after that our floor got swamped and we had a waiting room full. I wasn't tripping, though, because it made the time go by faster and before I knew it, it was time to clock out.

Even though I'd been there for a while it still felt good to get off and not be dog tired or sore from doing the work of two. After promising my sister I'd be ready in an hour, I drove home, only checking my phone one time. Of course, Dinero still hadn't hit me back and I was still slightly disappointed even though I'd made plans. As fucked up as it sounded, I would've ditched them hoes with the quickness to spend time with him instead, but since he was clearly too busy I was going to take them up on their offer.

Just like I'd promised I was showered and dressed within an hour, in a black scoop-neck jumpsuit, my Pine Green Black Retros, and a matching cropped letterman jacket. My hair was already done in a very natural thirty-inch Brazilian, so I didn't have to worry about it, and I kept my makeup simple, opting to just wear some lashes and Fenty gloss. I was adding a pair of small gold hoops to match my watch, when my phone lit up and Camille's face popped up.

"You better had been ready or yo' ass was gone get left!" she cackled as soon as the call connected, and I could hear Noelle's ass in the background talking shit too.

"Both of y'all can kiss my ass! I don't even be takin' that long." The lie had them both cracking up, and I sucked my teeth.

"Lies! All lies, but we outside so come on!" she hollered, hanging up in my face.

Ratchet ass bitch! I finished up and grabbed my little clutch that I was planning on wearing and switched out the door. As expected, my bitches were looking good and matching my fly, even though we hadn't discussed a theme for the night. Camille had on a cream crop top with the words dump him across the chest, some matching joggers, and the nude Yeezy slip-ins, while Noelle wore a gray two-piece leggings set with a black, white, and gray flannel around her waist and a pair of OG Shadow 2 Retros. It was going to be a chill ass girls' night and I was all for it.

When we finally made it, there was barely anybody there so we decided to drink and play a couple of games. Since those heffas had talked so much shit, I wanted to start with bowling first. I whooped their asses in a couple games before we moved on to something else. My phone finally went off with a text notification while we played giant Scrabble, and despite not wanting to be pressed I damn near dropped my drink trying to get to it. As soon as I saw Bae with the heart eyes emoji, I had mixed feelings. I was real-life torn between making him wait for a response like he'd done me and giving him a piece of my mind. Eventually, I just put that I was out with the girls, not even acknowledging his apology, and he hit me right back asking where we were. I polished off my drink while I squinted down at the screen, debating on if I should tell him or not. Did he even deserve to know after ignoring me all day?

"Hellooo, Ca'Mahri! You're the one who picked this old lady game and you're not even paying attention!" Noelle fussed over the music, and I knew her ass was already tipsy. Camille wasn't into it either and was furiously texting on her phone, probably arguing with Cash. When Noelle noticed, she rolled her eyes and pouted. "See naw, 'cause y'all both textin' y'all niggas instead of enjoying girls' night! I knew I should've dressed up so I could catch me one too!"

Camille's head instantly snapped up with her nose crinkled in disgust. "Who? I don't got no nigga, bitch, especially not Cash's thot ass! Fuck type of nigga be taking bitches down with their maid? Ain't no nigga of mine doin' that weird shit!"

"Arnold Schwarzenegger." Noelle shrugged, downing one of the shots we had lined up.

"What?"

"You asked what type of nigga be fuckin' his maid and I said Arnold Schwarzenegger. He had a whole baby with his maid, so it ain't that uncommon. Your real issue ain't even about that old shit, be honest, hoe. You were looking for anything to stop fuckin' with that man over." She said what everybody had been thinking, and Camille's mouth dropped open.

"Uhh, that crazy bitch violated me because of the shit they had goin' on!" Camille fumed, pointing a finger into her chest, and despite how serious she was trying to sound, me and Noelle cracked up. "Nah uh, I know you don't agree with this bitch?" She turned to me, and I hunched a shoulder and lifted my drink.

"I meeeean..."

"Y'all hoes unbelievable," she gasped, folding her arms over her chest.

"Naw, *you* unbelievable. Stop acting like you're that upset about some head. Clearly that hoe was tryna break y'all up and you fell straight for the bait. Now she over there all alone with yo' nigga 'cause you're scared of commitment." Noelle had just said a mouthful and I couldn't deny that it was all facts. I could understand if she really felt violated by Maria, but just like Noelle had said, she really was just afraid and subconsciously looking for a reason to leave Cash alone before she got too deep.

"Tuh! Well tell me how y'all really feel," Camille grumbled.

"And is!" The two stood glaring at each other, fueled by a bunch of liquor, and I knew we needed to move the fuck on. Playing referee, I suggested we go ahead and get some food, hoping that it would sober us up some. That instantly smoothed things over and by the time we were seated and munching on cheese sticks they were laughing and joking again.

We were still waiting on our meals when a group of three niggas walked by and slowed to a stop. I couldn't lie, they were all fine as hell and obviously took pride in their appearance, from their fades down to the shoes on their feet, but I wasn't mad enough at Dinero to entertain another nigga. Camille, on the other hand, had no problem taking the leader of the group to sit next to her while Noelle did the same. The last man standing eventually dropped into the seat next to me when I still hadn't offered it. He started making small talk and although I wasn't being downright rude, I wasn't being friendly with his ass either, so he quickly got the hint and buried his face in his phone.

"I'll be right back y'all." I excused myself and went to the bathroom, in hopes that by the time I returned them niggas would be gone. I spent the entire time primping in the mirror before washing my hands. Tossing my paper towels, I went to leave out and ran straight into a hard body.

"Ugh, watch where yo—" My words were cut off at the sight of Dinero standing there looking sexy as hell in a baby blue, collared shirt with the sleeves rolled up to his elbows and a pair of black slacks. It was obvious that he'd just come from the office and my week ass instantly got butterflies. "H-how did you know I was here?" I questioned, making him give me that cocky ass smirk he loved so much.

"I saw Noelle's Instagram story. Why didn't you tell me when I asked?" He leaned against the wall and cocked his head, awaiting my answer, while I inwardly rolled my eyes at Noelle's slow ass. I couldn't really be upset with her considering that she didn't know I was trying to give Dinero a dose of his own medicine, but still. Lifting my arm, I checked the time on my watch for dramatic effect.

"Uhhh, I texted you forever ago and you're just now getting back to me."

"I was busy, bae," he groaned.

"I was busy too." I shrugged, causing him to frustratedly run a hand over his head, and I realized he was due for a cut. I'd never seen him without a fresh lineup, so the sight of growing curls instantly caught my attention and let me know that he hadn't found the time to get in his barber's chair. That had me feeling slightly guilty for pressing him the way I was when he barely had time for himself let alone me.

"I'm tryin', Ca'Mahri, you gotta give me credit for that shit. I'm being pulled in so many directions right now but I make as much time as I can for you." It was on the tip of my tongue to mention how he wouldn't be so stretched thin if he hadn't added Tania's care to his list of responsibilities, but I knew how childish that would seem. "Come on, I'm here now. We can at least still eat and have a couple drinks before I take you home and fuck the shit out you."

Even if that didn't deflate my attitude it damn sure had my pussy thumping just thinking about him between my thighs. He reached out for me and when I didn't immediately move closer, he pulled me to him. With his arms around me and his dick pressed up against my stomach, coupled with the how many drinks I'd had, I was instantly ready to cave.

"Okay," I whimpered lowly, and his face split into a wide grin before he dropped a kiss on my lips. It didn't make any sense how easily I turned into putty in Dinero's hands. Breaking the kiss, he gave my booty a tight squeeze.

"Ayite, let's go chill with our people." He laced his fingers through mine and was already trying to lead me back out to where me and the girls were sitting.

"Uhhh, our people?" I quizzed with a raised brow.

"Yeah, Cash and my nigga Snoop came up here with me." He clearly didn't know why that shit had me on edge, but I was already preparing myself for the drama if Cash's crazy ass caught them niggas at the table. Shit, I was surprised I couldn't hear them arguing from where we stood. Either way, my grip on Dinero's hand tightened and I tried to brace myself for the bullshit.

CHAPTER SIX
CAMILLE

I rolled my eyes, regretting having agreed to these niggas sitting down after Don flashed the knot of money in his pocket for the third time. If it was one thing I couldn't stand, it was a flashy nigga, and his ass was definitely flashy. I'd already been able to tell that it was a bunch of dollar bills with a couple hundreds on top, which made his flaunting even more pathetic. Even Noelle had a bored look on her face from whatever his friend was saying to her. At this point my buzz was beginning to fade from being in their presence.

"Aye, you gone eat that?" he asked, already reaching his filthy hand in my cheese sticks, and I turned my nose up in disgust. I didn't play about my food, so I was ready to go clean off on his dumb ass. I was so busy mugging him that I didn't notice Cash approaching until Noelle kicked me under the table.

"What's good, Camille? Funny seeing yo' ass here, and with another nigga too! You on yo' City Girl shit, huh?" The smirk on his face would've given the impression that he was in a good mood, but I knew him better than that. He was there on straight bullshit, and I tensed up waiting to see what he was going to do. His ass had already been texting me asking who I was with not too long ago, and since I'd basically cursed him out I knew this visit wasn't going to be pleasant.

"Cash," I snorted, not wanting him to know how nervous he had me.

"You was tryna shoot yo' shot, huh?" He put his attention on Don, who looked confused about how to respond.

"Who me?" His voice raised an octave, and my lips twisted at how fast he'd bitched up. "Naw, I'm just over here while my homie holla at her girl." This nigga was marshmallow soft and it took everything in me not to call him out just to see Cash whoop his ass. Noelle's ignorant ass instantly busted up laughing, and I shot a look her way.

"Right." Cash chuckled like a psycho. "But just for future reference, I'm the only muhfucka tastin' that pussy! And since that's out the way, all y'all can get the fuck on. Best friend ain't tryna talk to none of y'all scary ass niggas either."

"Cash!" My mouth dropped open. This nigga just said whatever he wanted to whoever he wanted, and I wanted to slap the smug grin off his face.

"What?" He tossed his hands up, clearly amused as the guys all got the fuck out of dodge. Noelle thought the whole interaction was funny and hadn't stopped snickering yet. Unbothered by my irritation, he took the seat Don had just vacated, and his silent friend dropped next to Noelle with his face buried in his phone. That bitch instantly took notice. "Oh, my bad, best friend, this my nigga Snoop. Snoop, this Noelle, you can't call her best friend."

Snoop barely lifted his head to greet her and I knew she was feeling some type of way about it, but I was more focused on the looney toon that was sitting next to me. Even though I had an attitude about him putting my business out there, I was glad that he'd been able to get Don away from our table at least. Looks had definitely been deceiving in that situation, because I would've never thought that somebody who carried themselves well was a whole bum underneath it all. He probably would've copped an attitude if I had told him to move around, and more than likely we'd have been arguing and he would've ended up maced.

Stretching his arm across the back of my chair, Cash moved in closer and I quickly brushed his ass off. "I know you ain't mad about me gettin' dude broke ass out yo' face? Let me find out." He leaned back, giving me a funny look.

"Nigga, I couldn't care less. I do got a problem with you tellin' everybody and their mama about what we *used* to do in the bedroom though," I argued, making his forehead bunch.

"Shiiiit, it's true, and I was just suckin' the soul out yo' pussy a couple weeks ago. If you want, I'll come over and get you right after we leave here." His tongue darted out, wetting his bottom lip, and I squirmed in my seat. Cash definitely did things to me that had me still feeling aftershock days later. Hell, it'd been weeks and I could vividly remember the way he tongue kissed my coochie, and apparently she could too, because she was already throbbing in anticipation. He quickly caught on to the effect he was having on me and grinned widely.

"Nope! You ain't gone trick me with that weak-ass pull-out game." I shut him down. After taking a pregnancy test and popping a couple of Plan B's just to be sure, I wasn't as mad about what had happened the last time I fucked him. I was still going to the doctor, though, in the next week for a checkup, because there was no telling what his nasty ass was doing.

"You can't blame me. If anything I should blame yo' ass 'cause yo' pussy shouldn't be so good," he said with a disgruntled look on his face, like I was really the one at fault, and I couldn't do shit but shake my head.

"You know what? Where's Kash at while you out here sexually harassing me?" I changed the subject, realizing that I hadn't seen him in a couple of weeks.

"Maaaan, his lil' ass with my mama. She been monitoring Vernique visits and shit," he said like it was no big deal, but I was completely surprised. His baby mama had been MIA this entire time and now that she was back, I didn't know how to feel.

"Hmmm, when did she get back?" Something in my voice had him eyeing me, and I could tell that he was choosing his words wisely.

"She popped back up a couple weeks ago acting like she wanted to just pick right back up where she left off, but I ain't really feelin' that shit. That's why she only gettin' supervised visits for now." Suddenly, I felt bad for him. I damn sure didn't fuck with deadbeats and regardless of his ways, he was far from it. His baby mama, on the other hand, even though I hadn't met her I didn't like her and knew that if we ever crossed paths I'd beat her ass, whether me and Cash were together or not.

"Well, is Kash happy to see her at least?"

"Kinda, but he's still lil' so he's excited about everything. My mama said he asked about you when she was around and had her ass salty as fuck!" he laughed.

"I do need to come see my lil' man."

"You come home with me, you can see him all you want. You ain't even gotta worry about Maria 'cause I been got rid of her." His slick ass threw out there like I wouldn't catch on to the fact that it was getting too late for a toddler to be up visiting with anybody. Finding out that his live-in hoe was gone made me feel a little better, even though she should've been fired. I didn't want to admit it, but Noelle was right about. I'd never say it out loud, but Maria wasn't the first bitch to stick her tongue in my coochie, but that was another story for another day. She'd been let me know they'd fucked around to an extent by how she'd been acting since the first day we met, but when she saw that hadn't scared me off, she resorted to sneaking in our bedroom. In the back of my mind, I'd been waiting on the other shoe to drop when it came to Cash, and that was just what I needed. I shrugged, even though I already knew I was going to leave with his black ass, just as Ca'Mahri and Dinero appeared out of nowhere.

"I'll think about it." He sat back, satisfied with my answer, as Ca'Mahri looked between the two of us apprehensively. *Scary ass!*

"We bouta dip, Ca'Mahri just wanted to make sure y'all crazy muhfuckas was good." Dinero laughed and wrapped an arm around her shoulders. I could tell she hadn't been expecting him to say that, but her in love ass didn't disagree.

"Maaan, we good, don't nobody need y'all asses checkin' on us! Shit, we was just about to leave too! Come on, bae." Cash stood up dramatically, pulling me along with him, and Snoop did the same.

"Nah uh, so who takin' me home?" Noelle frowned, and I instantly looked at Cash since he was the one directing everything. We ended up deciding that we'd drop her and Snoop off since Dinero was going to Ca'Mahri's instead of to Winnekta where we were going.

After dropping off Noelle, we headed in the opposite direction where Snoop needed to go and as soon as we pulled up, it was obvious that something wasn't right. Cash brought the car to a slow stop and squinted up at the open door. Him and Snoop shared a look before he pulled his gun out from under the seat where he'd put it when we got in.

"Stay here, ayite, and if we're not back in five minutes then pull off."

"But—"

"Just fuckin' listen for once, Camille, damn!" he snapped, and my mouth clamped shut as he climbed out, followed closely by Snoop. Nervously, I climbed into the driver's seat and watched them enter the dark house. I kept my eyes on the door until various lights popped on, letting me know what part of the house they were in, and quietly urged them to come out because regardless of what he had said, I wasn't trying to leave without him. It seemed like it took forever before they finally came back out, and I breathed a sigh of relief. Cash paced on the porch with his phone up to his ear and I could tell just from his mannerisms he was mad as hell.

When he finally came back over to the car, the look on his face was a mixture of sadness and anger. I rolled the window down and he leaned in with his eyes on Snoop, who was still on the porch.

"I'ma have to get up with you later, bae. Somebody ran up in there and cleaned that muhfucka out." He sighed, letting me know this was a damn drug house, and even though he was omitting the obvious it was clear that people were dead inside. I was far from dumb about the shit that Cash was into, but knowing it and being there were two different things. Suddenly, I was worried for him if he was going to be staying somewhere that people were shot, and I instantly shook my head.

"No, I'm not leaving you here! How do you know they're not comin' back?" Headlights pulling up on the other side of the street stole my attention. "Nah uh, 'cause who the fuck is that!" I shrieked, ready to pull off with him still hanging in the window.

"Maaan, see this why you need to take yo' ass home, that's

just the cleanup crew. I called them niggas." He sighed. "Don't worry about me, I'm good out here. I got Snoop with me and Dinero on his way." I couldn't lie, that made me feel a little better and just like he said, a few niggas in hazmat suits stepped out and headed inside the house.

He gently turned my face back toward him and pressed his lips to mine. "Go home, I'll be there in a minute. I promise." Stepping back, he motioned for me to go and I slowly pulled off, hoping he was able to keep that promise.

By the time I felt him ease into my bed it was going on five in the morning, but I was just thankful that he'd actually made it. I snuggled my booty into him as he kissed on my neck and shoulder.

"Did y'all catch whoever it was?" I managed to moan out while he played between my legs. It didn't even take much and I was wet as hell.

"This ain't CSI, bae, them muhfuckas hidin' out, but I ain't tryna talk about that right now." He moved his hand up my stomach and squeezed my breasts as he filled me up, taking my breath away. "Damn."

He continued to kiss and suck on my neck while slowly grinding into me, and I quickly matched him stroke for stroke until we both came. I wasn't even going to snap on him for nutting in me again after the loss he'd taken. I kept my questions and judgment to myself as we hopped in the shower and washed each other, before fixing my bed and going to sleep.

CHAPTER SEVEN

CASH

After the shit that happened at the trap I was walking around more paranoid than usual. They hadn't even really got away with shit because Snoop had already done the drop, but they had managed to take out three niggas from our team, which was the bigger issue for me. Of course, we promised to take care of their expenses and give something to their families, but I still wanted blood. I had a few leads that might have been dumb enough to pull such a violation, and Lox was right at the top considering the shit he'd pulled not too long ago. Not only had we embarrassed him, but we'd stopped him from eating. Starving would have niggas doing suicidal shit, like trying to go up against me and my brother.

My first order of business was locating Walt, since he'd been the one who even brought that nigga Lox around. Him being MIA only further proved my theory that it was them. Even his baby mamas were in the wind, and I could only assume it was to keep his location from getting out. That was cool, though, because the harder I had to look for them niggas the worse their punishment was going to be.

"You know, Vernique's been asking about when she's gonna be able to take him home," my mama mused, snapping me out of the daze I was in and instantly blowing me. Dinero's bitch ass just tucked his head and kept eating like he hadn't heard her, knowing she was about to try and come down on my top about this shit. We were over there waiting on my pops so we could do a conference call with the plug, and I was wishing he'd hurry the fuck up because this was the last conversation I was trying to have. My mama was the type to be on the woman's side, especially when kids were involved, so I already knew she was about to plead Vernique's case.

Shaking my head, I pushed my food around some before saying. "I don't know what she doin' that for, he straight where he at."

"Is he?" she countered, and I could feel her staring a hole in the side of my face from across the table, making me finally lock eyes with her.

"Hell yeah! He get everything he need over here and ain't nobody over here just gone up and leave him for weeks on a whim!" I snapped, slamming a fist on the table. My outburst had Kash looking up from his iPad in alarm, and I quickly tried to pull myself together. The truth was I knew how easy it was for a court to side with a mother, and I damn sure wasn't trying to take it there and have them putting my son in Vernique's irresponsible care just because she'd birthed him.

"You better calm the fuck down talkin' to my mama, nigga. The fuck wrong with you?" Dinero grilled me, and I released a heavy sigh.

"My bad, Ma, I just don't think with his mama is where he needs to be after the shit she did."

"That's understandable, Cash, but what you need to

understand is that he don't need to be here all the time either. If you want full custody of him so Vernique can't just up and leave him, then you need to not be doing the same shit. You run the streets more than anybody I know, and Money is here with me while you do it. Now I'm not saying that I don't love my grandbaby, but if I wanted to be walking around with a baby on my hip, then I'd have one. You need to get your priorities in order and figure out how you're still going to be active in the business and be a single father at the same time," she chastised, with a raised brow. No doubt I'd been leaning on her a lot lately when it came to Kash, especially with Maria gone, but I didn't think she was gone get on my ass like that. She was straight up on her mama gotta have a life too shit, and now I had even more shit I needed to figure out. I tugged at my beard as she mugged me before finally agreeing.

"You right, Ma, I'm gone get some shit together, 'cause he ain't goin' back with V," I insisted, making her roll her eyes and get up from the table, taking Kash with her. I knew she was probably pissed about my decision, but if she had been on the phone that day when Vernique was talking all crazy, she'd definitely agree with me that he belonged with us.

"She gone fuck you up," Dinero's ass just had to add, shaking his head, as he went to put his plate in the sink.

"For what, not wanting his thot ass mama to raise him? You'd be on the same shit if it was you, so ain't nobody tryna hear that." Frowning, I dumped the rest of the food from my plate and set it next to his.

"I definitely would, but I'd also be spendin' time with him, or at least have a girl that could keep him while I'm workin'." I didn't know how serious he was, but it damn sure brought Camille straight to mind. She already fucked with Kash heavy, so it wouldn't be shit for her to fill that mother role.

My pops ended up coming down so we could handle the

call with our Mexico plug, Tino, and iron out a few details for our shipment. We piled into his office just as the phone rang, and he dropped into his chair and put it on speaker.

"Tino, how you doin'?" Pops asked, sounding way more upbeat than he looked. My old man didn't like issues with the business just like I didn't, so the recent death of our workers had him on edge.

"Ahhh, not too good, hermano. Why didn't you tell me about the trouble you've run into recently?" That had me sitting up in my seat as Pops locked eyes with me and Dinero. He quickly went from leaning back in his chair to scooting up and steepling his hands on his desk.

"We had a minor issue, but I wouldn't say it was trouble. It wasn't even worth mentioning, to be honest."

"I'd say somebody knowing the inner workings of your business was a big deal, regardless of how little they walked away with. You of all people should know that, Kendrick. This doesn't affect our dealings, but I did bring it up because I need you to handle this before our next conversation. Small things can become big things in a matter of months, if you know what I mean." Tino had basically just threatened us in so many words, and I was livid. I clenched my jaw and shared a look with my brother as my pops continued the conversation. Just like always, our drop was at a different location than the last time, set on the last day of the month, but the only thing on my mind was the threat he'd made. Having the possibility of our supply drying up put even more pressure on our backs to find out who'd ran in our shit and kill them.

"Well, y'all heard him," my pops spoke as soon as the call disconnected. "We need to handle this shit, ASAP. Find them niggas and end this shit," he said angrily, dismissing us with a wave of his hand. I was already thinking of sending somebody to Wisconsin to look for Lox's lame ass on my way out and had my phone in hand, ready.

"Dinero, you stay, I need to holla at you about Tania." Dinero sighed and did an about face, knowing Pops was going to chew his ass out. I'd been waiting to be a witness to what he had to say about that situation and was tempted to stay, but I already needed to get on top of that other shit. Instead, I dialed up our tech guy, Mason, on my way out the door to see if he would be able to get some type of trace on Lox or Walt.

I was on my way to the car lot, when I got a call from Snoop about Russ's house coming up short. After we had to shut shit down at his regular spot, I'd moved him over there and them niggas had been bumping heads ever since. I knew it was mostly because Snoop was serious about his business while Russ slacked a lot. This wouldn't be the first time his team had fucked up, but I was hoping with a go getter like Snoop around it would be the last.

I pulled up to the trap and checked my gun before getting out just in case I had to kill me a nigga. As soon as I stepped on the porch I could hear Russ inside fussing like a bitch while hypes stood around outside waiting to be serviced. I made them move around before letting myself in, and as soon as I stepped into the living room everybody jumped up to make it look like they were doing something. From where I stood I could see Russ pacing around the dining room while Snoop sat at the table with a bored expression. He peeped me first and then rolled his eyes over the raging man still stomping around like a kid.

"Bruh, I don't care about nothin' you sayin'. Plead yo' muhfuckin' case to Cash, nigga," he said smoothly, not alerting him that I was there.

"And I will, lil' nigga! My shit been runnin' just fine before you got here, now all of a sudden we short! I don't even know why Cash and nem put yo' young ass over here in the first place. You couldn't even handle yo' own shit!"

"I put him here 'cause I wanted to, nigga, now what?" I stepped up, making my presence known, and Russ instantly froze looking like he'd seen a ghost.

"C-Cash, man, I wasn't sayin' it like that," he stuttered, glancing from me to the gun in my hand. I wanted to shoot his ass just for all the shit he'd been talking and for letting a nigga that was barely old enough to buy liquor get him all worked up. His actions were looking suspicious as hell at the moment and I didn't like that shit at all. Squinting, I stepped further into the room and took a seat on the table.

"Oh really? It sounded like you was questioning my moves when you need to be questioning how yo' shit came up short, nigga." I glanced back with a raised brow. "How much they missin' Snoop?"

"A lil' over twelve racks."

"Damn, twelve, and instead of double checking you in here whining like a bitch in front of your workers while fiends sit outside making shit hot." It was more of a statement than a question, but even saying that shit out loud had me heated.

"My people solid, man, it wasn't no need to double check, and if some shit is missing he probably took it!" he argued, pointing at Snoop, who was still sitting relaxed like he wasn't being accused of stealing. My finger instantly began to twitch against the trigger as this nigga dug himself into a deeper hole.

"See, when you dealin' with another nigga money, shit like that don't fly and unfortunately for you, you talkin' 'bout *my* shit! Now either you find out where the fuck my money at or you gone catch a bullet right along with whoever was in this bitch stealing!" I stood to my full height and moved into his personal space. "You got until I come back tonight, nigga, no excuses!"

I was letting him off easy even though my first mind was telling me to splatter his shit now and save myself the trouble later, but I wasn't trying to shut down another house because I went on a rampage. Real shit, Dinero would've been proud.

"Matter fact." I stopped at the doorway and shot his dumb ass in the shoulder, instantly making him buckle. He was rolling around, crying, and hollering like a bitch, but my only interest was him shutting up. "Man, shut up before I shoot you in the other one! Snoop, call Quita to come patch this nigga up and make sure he do what I said." Shaking his head at that pitiful nigga, Snoop got right on the phone as I left and headed to the car lot.

CHAPTER EIGHT
DINERO

As soon as I walked through the door I could hear Tania throwing up, and I blew out an aggravated breath. Bruno's big ass stood on the other side of the wall looking like he was about to get sick just from hearing that shit. I told him to go get some fresh air, while I went to check on her, and instantly regretted that shit. The smell was way worse than the sound and my stomach turned as soon as I stepped in the living room. I found Tania on the floor next to my couch with her head damn near inside of a small bucket while Brenda, the nurse I'd hired, rubbed her back. Seeing me enter, a look of relief washed over her face and I knew she was damn near ready to sprint out the door, but she completed the task. Once Tania was done, she wiped her mouth and then helped her back onto the couch, unfazed by Tania's leering.

"How she been today?" I winced, already knowing that she was too much for just one person, even with a muscle head nigga there.

"It's been a pretty good day. This is only her second time

throwing up, and she hasn't cursed me out yet." The older woman shrugged and placed a cold towel on her forehead.

"Y'all don't gotta talk about me like I'm not here! Ask me how I been so I can tell you that I feel like I'm fuckin' dying! My stomach feels like it's about to fall out my ass and my entire body aches, Dinero!" she wailed, sitting up and staring at me with pleading eyes. This was the same routine I dealt with whenever I came home, except sometimes she'd cry and others she'd be cursing me the fuck out. For as many drugs as I sold, I'd never been around a recovering addict, and I had to admit the shit was exhausting, in addition to the other shit I was dealing with. I really thought it would be easier to help her out in the comfort of my own crib, but I was starting to see that I wasn't equipped to deal with this shit.

"You already know I'm not gettin' you no damn drugs, T, so you might as well lay back and take a nap or something," I said sternly, and she rolled her eyes.

"I hate you! I never asked yo' black ass to bring me here! I never asked for your help!" she bounced to her feet and screamed as Brenda eased out of the room to go and clean out her bucket.

"Naw, you just asked me for some fuckin' change, right! You were on the streets beggin' and shit, why wouldn't I have helped you! This not even you talkin', it's the fuckin' monkey on yo' back!"

Looking her over, I could see that she still hadn't gained any of her weight back and I knew that was partially because she was throwing up damn near every meal. Her skin was pale and clammy looking even though the air was on full blast, and her hair was all over her head. I didn't know how, but she was looking even worse than she had when we'd run into her in New York and that shit was fucking me up.

"I don't know how you could be so judgmental when you sell the shit! I probably got high off some of your shit, Mr. High and Mighty! How does that make you feel, huh? You're just as much responsible for this shit as I am!" Her eyes watered and before I knew it, fat tears were running down her face. It was like clockwork at this point. Sighing, I pulled her thin body to me and hugged her, careful not to squeeze too tight for fear of breaking her fragile ass.

"I'm just trying to help, T. I love you so I'm trying to help you get better. This shit isn't because I wanna hurt you, I just want you to get back to the Tania you were before this shit." She broke down in my arms as I stroked her hair. My pops had already warned me that this shit was going to be hard on me both mentally and emotionally, but being the type of man I was, I figured I could handle it. However, every day it was taking more and more out of me. The only time I even remotely got good sleep was when I stayed at Ca'Mahri's, and even then I was still worried about Tania. It was clearly time to start looking for an inpatient program for her where they would be better able to handle the mood swings and everything else that came with this shit.

Once I got Tania settled down and in her bed, I went and showered the day off, enjoying the way the powerful shower-heads kneaded the tense muscles in my neck and back. I had a lot of shit on my mind and it seemed like it all needed my attention at the same time, which wasn't possible even for me.

I spent over a half hour in the shower before I finally stepped out feeling a little bit more relaxed than when I got in, and after throwing on my briefs and some sweatpants, I rolled me up a blunt while I Facetimed Ca'Mahri.

"Hey you!" she gushed cheerfully, with her chubby face filling up my phone screen, and it instantly made me smile. My baby was always in a good mood, and between her positive energy and the exotic weed I'd just lit, I was hoping it would be enough to put my ass to sleep.

"What's up, bae? What you over there doin'?"

"Studying. Well, trying to anyway." She rolled her eyes and the camera was moved off her face and flipped to a huge book in her lap, but I couldn't focus on shit but her thick ass chocolate thighs folded underneath. My dick jumped and I quickly had to adjust it as I puffed on my blunt.

"I don't know about that book, but them thighs lookin' good as fuck right about now," I said, feeling my eyes beginning to droop a little as the weed started taking effect. The compliment had her giggling and she put the camera back on her face.

"You should've been over here then."

"I was just there and you ain't have shit like that on. I got baggie sweatpants Ca'Mahri. How you gone wait 'til I leave to put on the sexy shit?" I was lowkey feeling played seeing the boy shorts that had her camel toe poking and a little ass tank top with no bra. As hard as she always tried to get me to stay, I was surprised she hadn't pulled this shit out of her little bag of tricks. Now my ass was relaxed, high, and horny, but too far away to get my dick wet.

"I mean, this is what's usually under my sweats, it ain't my fault you ain't reach inside to get to it," she flirted, wiggling her eyebrows, with her silly ass.

"Ayite, don't say shit when I just start putting my hands in yo' shit." I wasn't even playing either. I'd quickly become addicted to Ca'Mahri and already found any reason to sink into her walls whenever I could. The last thing she should've been trying to do was put a battery in my back when it came to getting the pussy.

I finished the last of my blunt and laid back on my memory foam pillows, holding the phone at an angle so we could still see each other. Sleeping in Ca'Mahri's little queen bed had made me forget how comfortable my shit was, because I was already on the verge of closing my eyes, or maybe I was just that tired.

"You look sleepy as hell, Dinero," she noted, shifting so that she was now laying down too, but I knew she wasn't about to take her ass to bed yet because her overhead light was still on.

"I am, shit was a little crazy when I got home."

Her dark eyes softened as she quietly asked, "How's she doin'?" The concern on her face showed that she was genuinely wanting to know and not on no funny shit. She'd been asking about Tania every time we talked and I appreciated it. Most women wouldn't have given a fuck one way or the other, but Ca'Mahri wasn't like that. Especially since I'd blessed her with the dick.

I blew out a deep breath. "Same ole, same ole." I wasn't ready to tell her that I was about to fuck around and let some professionals handle things. I was already feeling bogus as fuck for just thinking about it, but it needed to be done. Not wanting to bother her with everything that was going on, I told her about her being sick and still not gaining weight, but left out the part when she cursed my ass out.

"Well, you're doing more than others have and that's gotta count for something," she told me once I finished. I wasn't usually a pillow talking ass nigga, but I found it hard to keep shit from Ca'Mahri. She knew everything I did about what happened with Tania, because I didn't want to keep her in the dark. Nodding, I tried to let her words bring me some solace, but I was still plagued with guilt. A few minutes later we wrapped up our call and I promised to stop by the next day.

I jumped up out of a restless sleep to the sound of my alarm going off, and I instantly snatched my gun off the nightstand. Even though our shit was built like Fort Knox there was always a chance that somebody could get onto our property, so I had a full alarm system with cameras and everything. I rushed out of my room and went straight to the one across the hall to make sure Tania was good, but her bed was empty, throwing me into a panic. Moving through the dark, I made my way down the stairs to find the front door wide open, and I ran outside without stopping for shoes. Since the alarm had woke me right up, Tania hadn't been able to get far, and even barefoot I was able to easily catch up with her.

"Get off me! Let me go! Help! Help!" As soon as she felt my arms around her, she started screaming like a damn fool, and my jaw clenched tightly.

"It's me! Calm yo' ass down!" I grit, hoping she'd quiet down once she heard my voice, but that didn't do shit but have her fighting harder and screaming louder. By now I could see lights beginning to cut on in my parents' crib, but I kept walking until I was home. With her still tightly in my grip, I shut the door and disabled the alarm. I took her back up to her room and shut the door to try and muffle her screams while I went to answer my ringing phone. I knew off top it was either the alarm company or my pops trying to figure out what the fuck was going on. It turned out to be the alarm people and after letting them know I was cool, I dropped my head in my hands. A few minutes later, Tania was still yelling at the top of her lungs to the point that I was ready to chloroform her ass, but I decided to answer the door instead. I already knew it was my pops, and there wasn't any point in making the old man wait.

"I take it that shit outside was Tania," he said, already knowing the answer, with his smart ass. Just like me he could hear her upstairs acting a fool and tearing shit up since screaming wasn't working. He stepped inside and glanced at the ceiling as some shit crashed, before bringing his eyes back to me.

"Yeah, T was tryna make a break for it." I sighed and ran a hand down my waves. "I got her before she got too far though."

"Son, I didn't come over here to lecture you or no shit, but we talked about this. As much as you care about Tania—hell, *we* care about Tania, you're not equipped to handle her care. She's gonna fuck around and hurt herself or you trying to chase that high and then what, all this shit would've been for nothin'. You're gonna have to put her in inpatient. You can't keep doin' this to yourself."

"Ayite man, I'ma look up a few places and then I'll take her," I finally said. I wasn't sure what type of facility was going to be able to take care of her, but I was hoping it was one that wouldn't let her sign herself out. My pops nodded and patted me on the back.

"Good, now let me go handle this real quick so we can get some fuckin' sleep." He pointed up the stairs to where we could still hear Tania wailing and tossing shit around, and pulled a syringe out of his robe pocket. My eyes bulged and I grabbed his arm to stop him.

"Aye man, you can't give her no fuckin' drugs!"

"You better get yo' damn hands off me, boy. This ain't no drugs, it's hospital-grade anesthetic! It's just gone put her crazy ass to sleep. Shit, do you need some?" he snapped, looking at me crazy. That instantly put me at ease and my grip on him loosened. He pushed my hand off of him completely and disappeared up the stairs with his face balled up. A few minutes later the house was dead silent aside from his shuffling feet as he came back down. "Take care of this shit, tomorrow," he stopped long enough to say before leaving out the front door.

CHAPTER NINE
CA'MAHRI

It was the day we had court for Walt's crazy ass baby mamas and I was nervous as hell. The last thing I needed was for these charges to fuck up either my job or school. I was fully willing to beg the courts if I needed to. Thankfully, Dinero had hooked us up with a lawyer friend of his, and I was hoping that he kept us out of jail and with a clean record.

"Bitch, relax, you're fidgeting so much you bouta make me nervous!" Camille slapped my arm and hissed like her ass wasn't already just as scared as me. She could talk all the shit she wanted, but the truth was she didn't want this shit affecting her job either. Sucking my teeth, I hit her heavy-handed ass back.

"Don't hit me, heffa, yo' ass is nervous too."

"Yeah, but I'm keeping it together, like you need to be," she chastised, just as our lawyer, Mr. Dossett, approached us. We both stood up so we could talk to him before going inside the courtroom. Pushing his glasses up on his nose, he ushered us to the side and grinned widely.

"Good morning, ladies, I just got word that neither Ms. Cole or Ms. Berry are in court today so the judge will probably dismiss the case," he told us, and we instantly started squealing excitedly, only for him to stop us. "We're still not out of the woods just yet because as you know, the state can pick up the charges. However, I feel like with you ladies' impeccable record and the fact that you're both in healthcare, they won't decide to." Even though he sounded confident, I still felt deflated. Everybody knew that the state's attorney was the worst and went out of their way to slam Black people every day.

After letting us know that we were next up, he excused himself to go talk to a colleague and I took a few calming breaths. I really wanted to talk to Dinero, but he was already busy dealing with Tania and I didn't want to add any extra stress.

Thankfully, only a few minutes went by before our case numbers were called, and we walked into the courtroom behind Mr. Dossett. He'd instructed us to dress our best, so I had on knee-length, nude dress with a thin, dark brown belt around the middle and matching nude heels, while Camille was rocking a navy blue, pinstriped pants suit, with a silk white blouse and black heels. Looking at us, you'd never think we were in court for beating some hoes up in the club, and that was exactly the look we were going for.

We stood at the podium quietly, while our lawyer went back and forth with the state attorney, who was an old, overweight white man. His ass was fighting for his life when he realized that the ratchet twins weren't there and tried to get a continuation, but the judge wasn't having it. The older Black man put me in the mind of Judge Mathis, because he wasn't for any of the nonsense, and he quickly dismissed the case even though the state did try to pick up the charges. As soon as he banged his gavel, we damn near ran up out of there and I silently thanked God for his mercy, promising to never get caught up in bullshit again.

"Ladies, it's been a pleasure, but please do stay out of trouble." Mr. Dossett grinned after we finally released him from the double hug we wrapped him up in.

"We will! Thank you!" we said at the same time, making him laugh as he walked off. "I knew we were gone beat that shit!" Camille's lying ass flipped her hair as we descended the steps outside. I looked at her sideways and rolled my eyes.

"What yo' lyin' ass bouta get into?" I asked once we reached the sidewalk. Since we were both off for court and I didn't have class, I was trying to go get some food before going home and resting.

"I'm going to see Kash and Ms. Keshia, you know it's been a lil' minute since I took my ass over there. Plus, I need to see Ms. Dorothea too... What?" her brows dipped when she saw my grin widening.

"I'm just happy that you're all in love again." I shrugged and her nose turned up as she gave me the finger.

"Tuh, ain't nobody said shit about love. Hell, I just started speaking to that nigga again!"

"Whatever Camille, see you later."

Instead of replying, her rude ass waved me off and headed in the opposite direction, walking hard as hell on her little kitten heels. I wasn't going to call her out about her feelings for everything Cash, but I did hope that eventually she stopped fighting him so hard. On the way to my car, I texted Dinero to let him know court went well. I wasn't expecting to hear back from him anytime soon but it just felt right to reach out to him.

I had a taste for Chick-fil-A, so I stopped through there on the way home and immediately caught an attitude seeing the long ass drive-thru line. Sucking my teeth, I pulled into the first parking spot that I saw and gathered my purse, before stepping out. Just like I thought, the inside was a lot less busy and I was quickly able to place my order. My stomach growled as I stepped to the side so the person behind me could order, and my cheeks flushed with embarrassment at how loud it was. The man looked right at me and smirked but didn't say anything until he was done ordering and came to stand beside me. His cologne quickly filled my nose and my brow raised in appreciation. I absolutely loved when Black men carried themselves well, and the tall, handsome stranger was definitely fitting the bill in a pair of black jean shorts that weren't baggy and a Bull's jersey with no shirt underneath, giving me a perfect view of his toned arms that were full of tattoos. On his feet were a pair of Jordan 1 mid Breds that looked fresh out of the box and matched his outfit perfectly. Even his dreads were neat and well kept, hanging down his back. He didn't have shit on Dinero, but I could admit that he was fine.

"I know you hungry, shorty, but stop staring at me like I'ma snack or somethin'," he said, catching me red handed as I stared all upside his head. My mouth fell open as I tried to think of something to say, when he laughed and put his hand out for me to shake. "I'm just fuckin' with you. My name's Lincoln, but everybody calls me Lox," he introduced, and I chuckled nervously, as I slipped my hand in his.

"Hey, sorry, I uh, I thought I knew you from somewhere," I lied, using my free hand to tuck a strand of hair behind my ear. "I'm Ca'Mahri." Flashing a perfect set of pearly whites, Lox eyed me from head to toe like he knew something.

"You know that's crazy, 'cause you look like a Ca'Mahri. I mean, it matches and shit," he said, and for some reason I got uncomfortable. I tried to shake the feeling as I pulled my hand away, since I'd literally just been staring at him a second ago, but something about his eyes wasn't right. Thanking him, I was glad that my order was up, and I wasted no time snatching it up. Not wanting to be rude, I managed to force out a farewell before damn near sprinting out to my car. I'd never experienced anything like that and the feeling didn't disappear until I was a few blocks away. The rest of the drive home I'd occasionally check my rearview, even though I knew nobody was following me. The shit was weird as hell. My ass definitely needed to cut down on the true crime shows while I was talking shit about Camille.

I grabbed my things and climbed out, noting how unusually quiet the block was. Normally, somebody was out from sunup to sundown every day, like my apartment was the damn 7/11.

"Cam." The deep voice startled the fuck out of me and I squeezed my legs together so I didn't piss on myself. After the initial shock wore off, I recognized Dinero making his way toward me and I sighed in relief.

"Whew, you scared the shit outta me!" I placed a hand on my chest as he came to a stop in front of me. His hands found my waist and he dropped a kiss on my lips.

"Not Tyson over here scared." He laughed and I shoved him away. Well, I tried to but he didn't budge. Now that he was around I was more relaxed, but I was going to keep what had happened to myself. I didn't want him to think I was crazy and I damn sure didn't want him to know I was in Chick-fil-A eye fucking some stranger. "You look good as fuck in this dress. This what you wore to court?" he asked, squeezing my booty as we traveled the short distance to my door.

"As a matter of fact, I did. Mr. Dossett told us that dressing up would help."

"I bet, shit. I would've let yo' ass off too if you walked in my courtroom wearin' this." His voice dropped and he pressed up against me while I unlocked the door. I could already feel his dick in my back, but he was going to be highly disappointed.

"Nope, don't even think about it. My period came on last night, so ain't no booty for you," I teased, bumping him back up off me.

"Shiiiiit, I ain't never been scared to run no red light. You see how hard my shit is, come on now. You gotta see it through, my boy."

"I wished the fuck I would! Nasty ass!" Sitting my food down, I wrapped an arm around his neck and stroked his beard. "Let me change outta this tight ass dress and eat, then I'll hook you up."

"Bet!" his horny ass quickly agreed and bit into his lip before sending me off with a firm slap on my ass. I'd learned that Dinero was an ass man and always found a reason to touch mine. I walked to the back, putting a lot more switch in my hips than necessary.

After handling my hygiene and changing into a comfortable two-piece lounge set from Fashion Nova, I headed back out and devoured my food while Dinero watched ESPN and occasionally took some of my fries. Once I was finished, I downed a bottle of water and went to rinse with Listerine so I could make sure that every remnant of food was gone.

I was sure that it only took me less than five minutes to do all that, but by the time I returned to the living room, Dinero was knocked out with this head resting against the back of the couch. A part of me wanted to wake him up with my lips wrapped around his dick, but I knew he needed his rest, so I snuggled up next to him and pulled a throw blanket over us. As soon as he felt my body, he pulled me closer.

"I love you, bae," he mumbled sleepily. and I swear my cheeks started hurting from how hard I was smiling. It was the first time that he'd ever said it, and even though it was subconsciously that only made it more authentic to me.

"Awww, I love you too!" I cooed, lifting up to kiss his jaw as my heart swelled in my chest. Besides the good news I'd gotten at court, this was the best part of my entire day. I felt like I finally had a nigga that actually meant it when he said he loved me, and I wasn't going to let him go.

CHAPTER TEN

CAMILLE

After I left my sister, I drove straight out to Winnekta feeling good as hell. Court had gone great and despite the shit that Cash had going on, we were vibing. Since I already talked to Ms. Keshia the night before about coming over, I had already stopped and grabbed her and Ms. Dorothea a couple things, which I lifted from the backseat after I parked in front of her house.

As always, when the maid let me in there was some 90's RnB playing over the surround sound and it had me grinning. Kash ran from around the corner and his eyes instantly lit up when he saw me.

"Amillle!" He looked adorable in his little t-shirt and basketball shorts with his hair loose and wild. I could really just eat him up.

"Kaaaaash!" I matched his energy, as he jumped into my arms and damn near knocked me over. Every time I saw him, he gave me baby fever and I had to check myself, because as cute as he was, I could still give him back. If I had a baby of my own that wouldn't be an option, so I always had to get my ovaries under control. "Hey, big boy, I missed you!"

"I miss you too!" His little strong ass squeezed my neck tightly as I carried him and my gifts into the kitchen where he'd just run from. I was surprised to see Ms. Keshia standing at the stove while their grandma sat at the table with her lips twisted like she'd just tasted lemon.

"Hey Ma, what you back there cookin'?" I asked, walking over and giving her air kisses, before setting her chocolates in her hands.

"Some bullshit!" Ms. Dorothea snapped from across the room, making me choke on a laugh, while Ms. Keshia gave her a stern look.

"Nah uh, don't be comin' for my food, old lady. This is the type of stuff you need to be eating anyway."

"Tuh, says who? I been feedin' myself my whole life and I'm still here, fuck around and die eatin' that shit!" the old lady fussed, crossing her arms over her chest.

"I'm not bouta play with you, Dorothea. You want me to go get Kendrick?"

"Girl, I wouldn't give a damn who you go get. I'll tell him the same thing I'm tellin' you, hell! If y'all tryna kill me for the insurance money, just say that!" My mouth fell open and even Ms. Keshia couldn't stop herself from laughing at that one.

"Anyway, thanks for the chocolate, baby. I'm making us a few *healthy* choices for brunch. I got some grilled chicken breast, summer salad, strawberry salad, broccoli, mashed potatoes, and corn." She pointed out the spread with a pleased grin, and Ms. Dorothea made gagging noises.

"None of that shit sound seasoned."

"Awww, Ms. Dorothea, it smells good. I'm sure out of all this food you'll like something. Plus, I brought you a gift too," I let her know, moving around the island so I could hand her the bouquet of white and yellow roses, with Kash still on my hip.

"I thank you, but why I couldn't get chocolates too? Least that way I'd have something to eat since I'm not bothering with that 'food.'" She gave me one of those smiles that a person gave to be polite even though they weren't happy.

"You have diabetes, Ma, you can't have chocolate, so it looks like you're gonna have to eat the same thing we're eating or a cold cut." The way Ms. Keshia said it, she didn't expect her to choose the latter, but that's exactly what she did.

"I'll take the sandwich for 500, Alex!" she said, making us all laugh.

Fifteen minutes later we were seated, making our plates while catching up. Since the strawberry salad had my mouth watering, I put a healthy serving on my plate and added the chicken on top after putting a little bit of everything on Kash's plate. He'd insisted on sitting next to me and promptly directed me on how he liked his food. Just like she'd said, Ms. Dorothea opted for a turkey sandwich and was now perfectly content.

"You gone eat all that, baby?" she asked, eyeballing my food.

"Yep, I'm greedy, Ms. Dorothea. I definitely don't play about food." I chuckled but was dead serious, and she squinted her eyes at me.

"Mmhmm," was all she said, but I knew her ass wanted to say something else. I was halfway through my plate when a commotion at the door caught our attention, and Ms. Keshia shared a look with her mother-in-law. After being with Cash at that damn trap house I must have got PTSD, because my heart was instantly pounding out of my chest, thinking somebody was coming for us. I immediately relaxed, though, hearing a woman's voice shouting.

"Ma! Maaaa!" Cursing under her breath, Ms. Keshia stood up but it was already too late, a woman stormed around the corner quickly followed by the Banks's maid.

"This bitch," Ms. Dorothea grumbled.

"I'm sorry, Mrs. Banks, I tried to tell her you were busy!"

"I don't need you apologizing for me! Keshia, you knew we had a visit today, so why y'all tryna keep me out! I know it's not for this bitch!" After her rant, I realized this was the infamous Vernique, and despite my clothes and our current location she was going to catch my hands and feet if she didn't watch her mouth. "Yeah, I'm talkin' 'bout you, bitch!"

"Vernique! Don't disrespect my mama and my house with this bullshit! Now I did forget that you changed the day this week, but that's not nobody's fault." Ms. Keshia was trying her hardest not to go off, but I was just running up a toll in my head and waiting for her to reach the magic number. Vernique was damn near foaming at the mouth as she looked from me to Ms. Keshia with narrowed eyes, not paying any attention to her son, and he wasn't paying her ass none either. He was still eating and playing on his iPad, which said that he was used to this shit from her.

"I just think it's funny that the day you forget, this bitch is magically over here eating lunch with my son! All y'all got me fucked up! Y'all not taking my baby and replacing me, nah, fuck that!"

"Ooh girrrl, I ain't gone be too many more bitches! I'm tryna be respectful, but don't get yo' ass beat in front of your son! I'm a whole animal under this suit!" I sneered, turning my chair around completely to face her.

Clearly, she was the type that was more bark than bite because aside from frowning up her nose and bristling, the only comeback she had was,

"Girl, ain't nobody scared of you!"

"Vernique, this is the reason why Cash isn't trying to let him go home, because of this crazy shit right here!" Ms. Keshia fussed, and I could tell that she was fed the fuck up.

"Please! We both know he's only acting funny right now 'cause of that bitch!" She barely had the word out before I was on my feet, while Ms. Dorothea's ratchet ass clapped excitedly. "You got them switchin' up on me, when you're the one who needs to get the fuck on!"

On some petty shit, I grabbed my chest. "What, and leave my stepson motherless?" I mocked, placing my hand on Kash's head and hugging it to me. That had her more angry than scared and she ran up on me with a growl. As soon as she was close enough I gave her a hard right and she stumbled back right on time to be caught by a bouncer-looking nigga.

With ease, he carried her out the room kicking and screaming out all types of threats, none of which I was scared of. I could've beat her ass with one hand behind my back and probably wouldn't break a sweat.

"Yesss! 'Bout time somebody knocked her on her ass! I been meaning to do it but I'll really hurt that lil' girl!" Ms. Dorothea cracked once me and her were alone. and I fell out laughing. Kash still hadn't paid either of us any attention and by the time Ms. Keshia came back, I had my giggles under control.

"I'm sorry about that, I—" She held up a hand to cut off my apology.

"It's okay. I know it's hard not to want to fuck her smart-mouth ass up."

"That's what I said!" Ms. Dorothea chimed.

We finished our food like nothing even happened after that and made plans to get together again later that week. Of course, Ms. Dorothea wanted to walk me to the door so she could talk her shit. She cracked jokes the whole way about me hitting Vernique and the lunch we'd had, but once I was standing out on the porch her tone grew serious.

"You know, I don't too often like the heffas these boys bring around, but you and your sister, y'all alright with me. I guess that's a good thing, though, considering." She shrugged and her eyes fell to my belly, instantly making my forehead bunch.

"Oh, well thank you, Ms. Dorothea, but ain't no babies over here," I denied with a firm shake of my head. This was the second time a Banks had said something to me about a baby and despite negative pregnancy tests and taking Plan B's, I couldn't help being a little shook. She gave me a look like I was stupid and rolled her eyes.

"You better go find out, girl. I don't want you to be like one of them girls who babies fall out into the toilet 'cause you're in denial." Petting my hand, she winked and backed away, slowly pushing the door closed. I was still stuck and unable to move for a second, but eventually I was able to shake off the weird-ass encounter and get behind the wheel of my car. I was glad my appointment was the next day so I could have it in writing that I wasn't pregnant to their crazy ass family. That thought had me looking down at the little bulge I had from eating so much, and I placed my hand there for a split second before snatching it right off. It was definitely time for me to take my ass home, and that's exactly what I did.

I was up bright and early the next morning ready to get my appointment over with. Fucking around with Cash and his grandma, I was more nervous than I should've been, but that wasn't going to stop me from finding out. Since I had insurance through my job that's where my primary was, and everybody spoke and was overly friendly when I came in. I kept finding something to nitpick about as I sat waiting to be called to the back, like how many pregnancy magazines they had and all of the women walking through with huge bellies. *Calm your paranoid ass down, Camille!* I chastised inwardly and logged on to Facebook to try and distract myself.

It wasn't long before I was called back and went through the normal process that I always did. I was done in an hour and waiting on my doctor to return, while I texted Noelle and Ca'Mahri in our group chat. I knew better than to tell them hoes what I was up there for because I didn't want to hear either of their mouths. Noelle would for sure think the shit was funny, and I wasn't in the mood for that shit. A knock at the door had me putting my phone away, and Dr. Angela Bennett stepped inside with a folder and a wide smile, instantly making my heart stop.

"Well, I guess congratulations are in order!" she squealed happily, and a bitch damn near fainted. I'd fucked around and got pregnant by Cash.

CHAPTER ELEVEN

CASH

After finding out that Russ was the one who'd been stealing, I finished that nigga off and gave his house to Snoop. He was definitely going to get them in order over there, and I was glad that was one less issue I had to worry about, especially since it was time for our shipment. I pulled up to the address that we were sent at the same time as Dinero, who was driving a food delivery truck. He stepped out and came over to the beater I drove and shook up with me before leaning against the passenger side door with me.

"Yo' ass been in the wind all day, nigga, where you been?" I questioned, putting my phone away since Camille's ass was leaving me on read. We'd been doing good and now it seemed like she was on some other shit after her and Vernique got into it. I was the first call V made when she left my mama's house, and her ass felt dumb as hell when I laughed in her face. The only issue I had was that I wasn't there to see that shit. She hung up on me after that and I tried to call Camille to check on her, but she'd been ignoring the fuck out of me. Since I had other shit to do, I didn't press the issue, but now it was going on twenty-four hours and I still hadn't heard from her bald-headed ass. After I handled this, though, I was going to pop up on her and find out what she was ducking me for.

"Shiiiit, I dropped Tania off at rehab. You know they gotta fill out paperwork and give tours and shit."

"I don't know shit, I ain't never been to no rehab!" I laughed and he sent a hard glare my way.

"Shut yo' goofy ass up! You know what I mean!" His ass sounded mad as fuck, but I knew that was only because he was feeling some type of way about sending shorty to crackhead jail. He should've really done it sooner and saved himself some stress, but I wasn't going to tell his sensitive ass that. I tossed my hands up as a truck approached and stopped with the headlights on us. It seemed like it took them forever to cut the lights off, but they finally did and then stepped out. Javi, Tino's man servant, came walking towards us, and I had to bite back the laugh I felt threatening to erupt. His ass already looked like a dead ringer for Danny Trejo except he was tall as hell and super buff. This nigga was clad in painter's coveralls that looked too damn small on his frame, and I could barely keep a straight face. Dinero elbowed me and grunted for me to chill, just as he reached us.

Without speaking, he held out the keys to his truck to Dinero, and my brother did the same. Once they switched, I waited until Dinero was safely inside of the truck before getting in my car and following him out to the warehouse. We both drove the speed limit and made sure not to switch lanes on the highway so as not to draw attention to us.

I breathed a sigh of relief and thanked the man upstairs once we finally made it without any hiccups. After Dinero backed the truck inside the two security guards we hired immediately began to unload it while we monitored. Once all the kilos were accounted for, we locked up and drove our own cars back into the city. I was headed to Camille's crib to find out what her problem was and even though he hadn't said it, I knew his ass was going to Ca'Mahri's.

When I pulled up, I parked right behind her car and made my way to the door while I called her. She still wasn't answering the phone for me, but she eventually came to the door after I knocked a few times. She looked surprised to see me, like she hadn't checked her peephole before letting me in, and I made a mental note to check her about it, but the sight of her phone in her hand stole my attention. I quickly snatched it up as I passed by her and went straight to her call log.

"Hey!"

She chased me behind me, trying to get it back, but I was able to easily keep it out of her reach. "I'm glad to see this muhfucka actually work since yo' ass been dodgin' me for damn near two days," I said slickly, trying to keep my temper under control. When she realized she had no wins, she folded her arms and just mugged me like I'd done something to her crazy ass.

"I needed some time to myself, is that okay with you?" Squinting, I took her in, trying to figure out just by looking if something was wrong with her. She looked exhausted or like she'd been crying, but other than that she didn't look ill at all, and now I was really curious. It seemed like she'd been acting funny ever since the fight with Vernique, so I could only assume that was the reason for the distance she was trying to create.

"Nah, you gone have to come better than that. Is this shit about what happened with my baby mama?" The mention of Vernique had her wincing, and I quickly picked up on that. "So, it is about Vernique?" I insisted, getting irritated, and she sucked her teeth and broke eye contact.

"This ain't got shit to do with yo' ugly ass baby

mama....well, not Vernique anyway." Confusion washed over me as she mumbled that last part.

"The fuck, I don't got no other baby mama! I know ain't no bitch told you she was pregnant!" Suddenly, the bitch Ashley from Walmart came to mind. I'd only fucked with her once when shit with me and Camille was bad and the pussy was trash, but she'd been blowing me up ever since. I just knew damn well she hadn't been going around saying she was carrying my fucking baby! Real shit, I got nervous thinking somehow Camille found out about that shit because even though we weren't technically together, I knew how women were.

"Ughhhh!"

She stormed off toward her bedroom and I quickly followed, ready to beg if I needed to. Stopping at her night-stand, she snatched something up and whipped around, pushing it into my chest. Right away I knew what I was looking at after seeing every single one of Kash's.

"I'm the other baby mama and I really wanna fuck you up!" she fumed, but I couldn't keep the smile off my face. I'd only been fucking with her when I said she was already pregnant, but apparently, I had spoken that shit into existence.

"I mean, it's here now so what you gone fuck me up for? We're bouta have a baby, damn!"

"Uhhh, I don't know about that," she grumbled, and for the first time I took my eyes off the little paper I was holding.

"What don't you know about? Our fuckin' baby?" I moved closer with a deadly look when she still hadn't answered me. She avoided my eyes, unfazed by the anger radiating off my body, and released a deep sigh.

"Yes, *our* baby! Should I be excited when you already got baby mama drama, and still runnin' the streets and havin' drug wars? Do that sound like some shit I wanna bring a baby into?"

"You're makin' excuses, bruh. Ain't none of that shit for you to worry about—"

"How the fuck is it not? All of that directly effects this baby and since I'm the one carrying it, then I'm the one who gets to make the decision about whether or not I wanna go through this shit with you for the next eighteen years!" Her voice was trembling and fresh tears threatened to erupt from her eyes as she said that crazy shit, but I was far from worried about her emotional state. Mainly because she was sounding selfish as fuck and I was trying to stop myself from hemming her up for saying all that hot shit. There had been a few times in my life when I was willing to let a bitch kill my seed. Shit, I had even considered it when I found out about Kash, but Camille having my baby felt different to me. I real life felt violated just thinking about her getting rid of this baby, and I knew I needed to get the fuck from around her before I said or did some shit I'd regret. Nodding, I clenched my jaw and stormed out of the room, trying to put some distance between us, but her goofy ass just followed behind me. I was doing good ignoring her as she called my name, but just as I reached the front door she grabbed my sleeve. Stopping in my tracks caused her to run into me, that's how close she was, and a look of alarm flashed across her face. Normally, I wouldn't want her to be afraid of me, but in this moment she needed to know not to fucking play with me.

"I need you to understand that if I find out you killed my baby, I'm gone put a bullet in yo' fuckin' head, Camille," I told her calmly like I was telling her something as simple as the time, and I could damn near see her heart beating out of her chest, which was good because that meant she knew I was serious. She opened and closed her mouth, but I didn't even wait to see what her ass was trying to say, I just slipped out the door.

It had been days since I'd left Camille's crib and I was still just as pissed as I'd been that night. I was hoping she'd take heed to the warning I gave her, but knowing her ass, she'd gone and did the shit just to spite me. It was a lot of shit I could look past, but if she'd killed my baby I'd never forgive her for that shit. The love I had for her had me conflicted on whether or not I'd be able to really go through with killing her. *Damn, was the shit I was feeling love?*

"You straight, bruh?" Dinero paused in the middle of stuffing the duffle bag he was holding and looked across the table at me with concern.

"Yep," I lied quickly. I wasn't straight, I was fucked up off weed and Hennessey, hoping it would take my mind off the shit, but it was only making me think about it more. Sitting the bag I was working on to the side, I opened up another and started loading it up.

"Yo' ass lyin', but why every time you go through some shit it's when we workin'? Ain't nobody tryna go behind you, fixin' yo' fuck ups 'cause you can't separate business from personal," he lectured, with his annoying ass.

"Nigga, I said I'm straight!" I didn't realize how fucked up I was, but the look on Dinero's face let me know that I'd let it slip. His eyes narrowed at me from across the table and his body stiffened.

"You fuckin' drunk, nigga!" he thundered, but I put my head back down and continued what I was doing. I wasn't in the mood for that big brother shit at the moment and was prepared to take it there with his ass if he got to acting stupid.

Unfortunately, he was with all the bullshit because he was in my face within seconds, smacking shit out my hand like I was a bitch.

"Man, get the fuck out my face, Dinero. I ain't fuckin' with you, man."

"I don't give a fuck! Why would yo' dumb ass come if you knew you was fucked up!" Grumbling, I waved him off, and he shoved my ass into a nearby chair while he got his phone out. I already knew he was calling our pops. I wasn't even that fucking drunk for him to be acting the way he was.

He got off the phone quick as hell and started going back through my bags while I mugged him evilly. I didn't appreciate him questioning me, like I hadn't been doing this shit for years. "That shit right, ain't it?" I quizzed, leaning forward with my elbows rested against my knees.

"That ain't the point. It's about more than just counting, nigga. You gotta be alert in case some shit go down. What if a muhfucka came in here bussin' and yo' wino-head ass too fucked up to protect yourself?"

"I ain't no fuckin' wino, goofy-ass nigga! I had some Henny and a couple blunts, like I always do!" Scoffing, I went to stand up, and he pushed me right back into the chair. "Man, you better stop shovin' on me!"

"Sit down then until Bruno can take you home. Pops gone come finish with me." Right then Bruno's beefy ass came into the room and just stood there next to me. "Gone with him, Cash, or do you need him to carry yo' goofy ass?"

"I'm a grown ass man, ain't no other grown nigga bouta carry me nowhere!" I jumped up and wanted to slap the silly ass grin off my brother's face, but instead I just headed out to my car. Dinero was on some other shit, and I needed to get from around him at the moment.

CHAPTER TWELVE
DINERO

My brother was tripping and I didn't know what was going on with him, but it had his ass falling off on business. Our pops had to pick up his slack the other night and I was having to get up with muhfuckas about Lox, who was still in the wind. The tech guy had been trying to get at that nigga and when he didn't answer, he called me to come view the tapes for the trap that got hit. Even though we had our suspicions, it was finally confirmed that Lox and that goofy ass nigga Walt were the ones who ran up in our shit. The little bit that they'd gotten away with was nothing and we definitely wiped our asses with that type of money, but I knew his weird ass wasn't done. So far, hadn't shit else happened, but I was trying to stay on alert just in case it did.

Tonight, I was taking a break from that shit though. As guilty as I felt for just dropping Tania off at rehab, I couldn't deny that it was a huge weight off my shoulders. I was getting more sleep, and I wasn't as stressed out. I made sure to check on her every day, since I wasn't allowed to talk to her just yet.

That was cool, though, as long as I knew she was getting the help she needed.

I pulled up to Ca'Mahri's crib to pick her up for a night out. It had been a minute since I'd taken her anywhere, and since the last time ended abruptly I was trying to make that up to her. She'd been doing her thing with school and work, and I wanted to show her that I was proud of her for what she was doing with her life.

"Damn, baby," was the only thing I could say when she opened the door. She was wearing the fuck out of a royal blue dress that had a plunging neckline and displayed her slim waist and thick hips. The two splits gave me a perfect view of her oiled up thighs and all I could think about was wrapping them around my neck. When I finally worked my way back up to her face, she was cheesing.

"I take it you like what you see?"

"Shiiit, I love it. I'm ready to say fuck the restaurant and just order in!" She laughed, but I was dead ass serious.

"Yeah ayite, you promised me fine dining and I plan on getting your money's worth." Leaning up, she puckered her red lips for a kiss, and the heels she wore made it so that I didn't have to bend down that much to oblige her. She smelled good as fuck too, like candy or something, and I slipped my arms around her waist, pulling her closer. It was crazy how open she had me. When she finally pulled away I just looked down into her face, mesmerized.

"Ayite, come on before I change my mind," I said, willing myself to let her go.

Once I helped her into the car, I held her hand over the console, occasionally bringing it to my lips as we drove. I had reservations for us at Cite, knowing she would love the fact that it rotated, and I wasn't disappointed. Her eyes lit up as soon as we entered the dining room and were led to a seat by the window.

The whole time she just kept staring out at the view, completely blown away, but we were halfway through our meal when she finally realized we were moving and I had to stop myself from laughing at the amazed look on her face.

"Dinero! Why didn't you tell me we were movin'?" she gasped with wide eyes.

"I thought you knew, girl, you been starin' out the window the whole time, shit!" Shrugging, I took another sip of my tequila while she looked back and forth between me and the window. After finding out, she barely touched her food she was so enthralled with the view, and I was unable to take my eyes off her.

When the waiter returned to clear our table, though, I finally looked away and of all the muthafuckas to run into, Tania's fat ass father was the last one I was expecting to see. Chicago was big enough that I hadn't managed to come across him in years; plus, we didn't run in the same circles, but as soon as I saw him I recognized him. He wasn't with Tania's mama, but a group of men that all probably had some involvement in the church and held him in a high regard despite the shiesty shit he did. I was staring so hard that I didn't realize Ca'Mahri or the waiter were trying to get my attention, until she reached over and touched my hand.

"Bae." I brought my hard eyes over to her and the shit had her flustered. "Uh, um, he wants to know if you want another drink," she said quietly, trying to read me, and I forced a smile to relax her.

"Yes, I'll have another one." I nodded, sending the older man on his way.

"Are you okay?" Her voice was uneasy still despite the front I was putting on.

"I'm cool, shorty." I gave her my attention and this time the fake-ass reassuring smile seemed to put her at ease. The rest of dinner I divided my time between her and Reverend Cox, careful to not let him or her catch me staring a hole in his face, and when it was time to leave she was none the wiser that I'd been planning a nigga's death while eating my chocolate hazelnut cake.

Hours later, after I'd fucked Ca'Mahri to sleep, I slipped out of her bed and put my clothes back on. I'd had Snoop come up to the restaurant and follow that nigga, so I knew he was holed up in a motel and not at home where he needed to be. I really should've just let Snoop put that nigga out of his misery and stayed in bed cuddled up with my girl, but this shit was personal. I was halfway to the motel when I got another text telling me that whatever woman he was with had left, and I pushed the pedal to the floor. Doing the dash got me from Ca'Mahri's spot to the musty ass room this nigga was in, and I met Snoop at the end of the parking lot away from the flood lights they had out there.

"What's up, you need me to go in with you?" he asked when I leaned into his car window, and he handed me a gun and ski mask. The little nigga was always on go and ready to put some work in. With no questions asked he'd stopped whatever it was he was doing to come and keep watch over the reverend, and I appreciated that shit.

"Naw, I got this one, you gone head out." He nodded and bumped my fist, before starting up his car. I didn't wait to see when he pulled off, I just pulled the mask down and headed to room 102, making sure the safety was off. Standing on the side of the door where he wouldn't see me, I gave a firm knock. I could hear the old ass bed creaking as he stood, and then his feet shuffling across the floor.

"I knew you'd be back, Betty!" The grin that was on his face when he swung the door open instantly fell upon seeing me, and I wasted no time slamming the butt of my gun in his shit. He fell back on the floor with blood shooting out, and I came all the way in the room, making sure to kick the door closed behind me. "W-what do you want! I have money!" he crawled backwards begging, but I quickly advanced on him.

"Shut the fuck up! Don't nobody want yo' money!" I kicked him in the gut, making him howl out in pain, before crouching down into his face. Lifting my mask, I smirked at him and his eyes narrowed in recognition. "Remember me?"

"Dinero!" he spat, looking at me in contempt. "What more do you want from me, demon? You already took my daughter and ruined her life!"

"No, *yo' ass* ruined her! Forced her into some shit she didn't want and then threw her the fuck away after the shit didn't go as planned. You supposed to be a man of God but you ain't very forgiving, huh?"

"I am a man of God! I dedicated my life to the church and my family, but we both know how the devil likes to come in and wreak havoc!" Wiping his nose, he sat up like shit was sweet, only for me shove the gun into his forehead.

"You callin' me the devil, nigga?" I grunted, more than ready to end his life. Not only had he killed my seed, but he'd pushed his daughter into the streets and left her there. As far as I was concerned, those were crimes punishable by death. He didn't deserve to lead a congregation and he damn sure didn't deserve to be labeled as the loving father when Tania finally returned in better health. Shit, the world was better off without niggas like him.

"I call it how I see it!" he sneered, trying to be tough, and that was probably only because he knew he had no outs with me.

"See you in hell then!" Despite all the shit he'd been talking, his eyes ballooned and I wasted no time sending a bullet crashing into his skull. His body fell back with a loud thud, and I pulled my mask back down before disappearing out the door.

Just like I expected, Snoop's ass was still sitting in the same spot waiting, and he pulled off with a nod once I was finally inside my own car. I took my time and drove the speed limit all the way to the bachelor pad we used for miscellaneous shit. It had been a while since I'd been there, but I was glad Cash still had clothes tucked inside. I stripped down to my underwear right on the porch and headed straight to the shower, washing every piece of evidence off my body. Once I was done and dressed in some black sweats, I packed up my bloody clothes and the gun inside of two garbage bags. I even brought a couple bags out and lined my front seat before driving back to Ca'Mahri's crib and disposing of the bag on the way.

When I finally stepped back into her bedroom it was going on four in the morning and I was glad her ass was still in there snoring. I didn't want to have to explain me leaving in the middle of the night, because there was no doubt she'd ask, with her nosy ass. I stripped back down to my boxers and slid in bed behind her, pulling her soft body close, and was out like a light.

The next morning she had to go to work, which was cool with me because I needed to get my car detailed ASAP. As soon as I kissed her and sent her ass on her way, I was headed in the opposite direction and dropping my shit off.

"Fuck you gettin' yo' car detailed for, nigga?" Cash wanted to know as soon as I climbed into his car, looking like he was in on some secret. I instantly regretted calling his ass, but I couldn't call my pops 'cause he'd definitely get on my ass about the reckless shit I'd done. "It wouldn't have shit to do with Tania's daddy being found dead in a motel, would it?"

"Mind yo' fuckin' business, Cash!" I grunted, and that only made him chuckle as he pulled off. Without me having to say, he already knew what was up, but with my brother I knew it was a no-judgment zone. His ignorant ass would crack a few jokes, but he wasn't going to tell me I shouldn't have done it. Not that it mattered what anybody said, the reverend deserved to die, and I didn't feel bad about it.

"Man, where yo' ass goin' 'cause I ain't bouta deal with yo' attitude!" He smirked, finding way too much humor in this shit.

"Take me home, I need to change and—"

"Speakin' of which, is them my muhfuckin' clothes, nigga?" Eyeballing me had his ass swerving into the next lane, but he quickly recovered and straightened the wheel back out. It was crazy that he even paid attention to shit like that, but leave it to Cash to know every piece of clothing he had even down to the regular shit. The joggers weren't even shit but a pair from Walmart and his ass was about to kill us over them.

"Man, I'll give you this weak-ass sweatsuit right the fuck back!"

"I don't want that shit back, I'll take my money though." He shrugged and my face instantly balled up.

"You pressed for twenty bucks, man?"

"Actually, it was $25.96." I just looked at his ass as he fell out laughing and turned onto our property. Even though he was getting on my nerves, I was happy to see him somewhat back to his usual annoying self. So, instead of roasting his goofy ass I sent a transfer to him for the exact amount he'd said and got out, slamming the door behind me.

CHAPTER THIRTEEN
CA'MAHRI

I cheesed as I looked over my first test, proud that despite my schedule and relationship I still managed to get an A. It definitely wasn't easy, but I was out here doing my thing and this was just one of the milestones on my journey. I quickly snapped a picture and posted it to social media, knowing my friends were about to run my likes up. The instructor dismissed the class and I gathered up my things to head out. Today was one of the rare days that I only had class and didn't have to work, which I was grateful for.

I quickly blended into the group of other students, speaking to a few of them on the way to my car. By now summer was in full swing so the sun was already kicking my ass as I climbed behind the wheel and blasted the air. The parking lot cleared out fast since it wasn't many of us picking up the summer classes, and I was one of the last ones pulling off. While I drove I called Camille and Noelle on three-way and put the phone on speaker.

"What's up, hoes, y'all wanna go to the lake front to cele-brate my A?" I asked as soon as they were both on the line.

"Oh shit, congratulations! You know I'm down, who bringin' the drinks?" Noelle was the first to agree, with her alcoholic ass.

"Congrats, boo! But ugh, the beach? Ain't nobody tryna be out in the hot ass sun!" Frowning, I looked at the phone like my sister could see me and sucked my teeth. She'd been acting funny as hell lately and never wanted to do shit outside of work. As far as I knew, things with her and Cash were doing okay, so I didn't know what her issue was, but I was tired of her being a Debby downer. Before I could ask, Noelle was already on it though.

"You don't never wanna do shit no more, bitch. What's been goin' on with you?"

"Why somethin' gotta be wrong 'cause I don't wanna go to busted ass Lake Michigan?" she scoffed, and I could hear her moving around.

"It ain't just Lake Michigan, hoe, it's the bar, the gamin' spot, the restaurant. Yo' ass been real antisocial, when you normally be with all the bullshit."

"What Noelle said," I cosigned, because everything she'd said was the truth. Over the last week Camille had refused to go anywhere aside from work for one reason or another, and every excuse she gave was weak as hell.

"Y'all hoes ain't bouta keep gangin' up on me!" she said around a mouthful of food.

"Nuh uh, we need to have an intervention. I'll meet you over there, Cam, and I'll bring this Casamigos, and don't be tryna leave either, Camille. I'm on my way now." Just that fast she hung up, and I rolled my eyes. Since she was bringing the liquor I would pay for us some food. I placed an order at the Chinese spot once I got home and quickly showered before putting on some gray biker shorts with an orange graphic tee. After slipping into my rainbow crocs I went to pick up the food.

By the time I arrived at my sister's Noelle was already there. She opened the door and shoved the bottle in my chest before I'd even crossed the threshold. "Here, you gone need this, bitch!"

"What—?"

"Just trust me," she urged, tilting the bottle up to my lips and taking the bag of food from me. That shit only had me more confused, but I did what she said as I followed her deeper into the apartment. Camille looked between me and the bottle before rolling her eyes. "Don't do all that, gone tell yo' sister how you fucked up our fuck nigga-free summer!" Noelle plopped down on the couch and waved her on. Now I was really puzzled and took another sip of the drink.

"You're doin' too much, I'm only—"

"Pregnant! This bitch done went and got pregnant! I thought for sure it was gonna be yo' ass but not my rodey!" This dramatic ass heffa fell back against the couch and covered her face with her arm, while Camille mugged her.

"Awww, that's all!" I cooed, running over to my sister and hugging her. "I'm gone be an aunty! Does Ma know? Wait, does Cash know?"

"Uhhh, first of all, both y'all heffas need to pump yo' brakes. I haven't figured out what I'm gonna do yet, but y'all wanted to know what was goin' on and this is it." My mouth snapped shut at her admission because I didn't know what to say. I didn't want to discourage her from doing what she felt was best, but I couldn't help being a little disappointed. Noelle, however, didn't seem fazed at all by it, and only turned her head to give her a look that said she didn't believe that shit.

"Bitch, please! Cash ain't about to go for that and you know it."

"This my pussy, he can't tell me what to do!" Camille snapped, clearly frustrated by the truth of what Noelle was saying. I didn't know if she had told him yet, but I was sure if he knew he was going to do everything he could to make her have that baby.

"Whatever you say, girl." Noelle brushed her off and reached for the food.

"Well, I'm behind you, whatever you decide. You do need to at least tell Cash though." I kneeled down next to her and pet her hand.

"Thank you, at least somebody being supportive."

"Bitch, I am being supportive. When you have the baby I'm gone be the best drunk aunty ever." We both shot Noelle's crazy ass a look.

"You're so damn annoyin'," Camille quipped while Noelle shrugged and kept making her plate, unbothered. I could definitely already see her ass giving the baby whatever it wanted behind Camille's back. I was for sure going to be the cool aunty though.

We spent the next few hours downing the Casamigos while my sister stuffed her face. It wasn't any different than how things normally were when we all hung out and I think Noelle noticed it too. Despite Camille's insistence, we landed on the topic of baby names and she tried to resist it for a while but eventually chimed in with the ones she liked. I could already see that even though she wasn't admitting it, I was going to have a cute little niece or nephew to spoil within the next year.

"You comin' over?" Dinero's deep voice filled my ear and I instantly shivered. He always had that effect on me even if we'd just seen each other. Smiling, I headed back inside since my break was over and shook my head like he could see me.

"I just left you this morning, sir, plus I don't know if I

wanna drive all the way back out there after dealing with these folks tonight," I admitted with a sigh as I stalled in the hallway. I was on the recovery unit and between the nurses and the patients having me running around, I was tired as hell. It was one of the harder days I'd had since working at Rush, but it was still a breeze compared to where I'd come from.

"I'll pick you up from home, just pack a bag for a couple nights." He didn't hesitate to come up with a solution, and I giggled at his thirstiness.

"Baaaae, I been at yo' house more than I been home. I might as well move in at this point."

"Shiiiiit, might as well," he said so quickly that my eyebrows shot straight up. I was being smart when I'd mentioned moving in, but I couldn't tell if he was joking or for real when he answered. Knowing Dinero, he was dead ass serious, but I was almost afraid to confirm my suspicions. After a pregnant pause, I finally found my voice.

"You know I was just jokin', right?" I even added a chuckle so that the moment wasn't so awkward, as I checked the time on my watch. There were only a few minutes left in my break and I still had to make it all the way to the time clock.

"I'm for real, though. You're over here damn near every night anyway and with the way gas goin' up it'll be more cost effective for us to just live in one spot." His explanation had me cheesing even more since he was using any excuse to get me to agree. It was cute and had only made me love his sexy ass more.

"We'll talk about it later. I gotta go punch back in before I'm late."

"Ayite, but we're definitely gone finish this." He sighed and suddenly a bunch of noise filled his background. "Aye, y'all niggas shut the fuck up, I'm on the phone! Man, talk to you later, bae. I love you."

"I love you too," I cooed, hanging up as laughter erupted on the other end. He seemed totally unbothered expressing his affection for me while his peers were around, and that was just another reason to love him.

Two hours later my shift was over and just like he'd said, Dinero was outside waiting for me. After riding to my apartment I packed me a bag while he went behind me throwing in more clothes, insisting that I would need them, then we headed out to Winnekta. As tired as I was, I fell asleep before he even got on the expressway and was shaken out of my slumber as soon as we arrived.

"Wake yo' slobbin' ass up," Dinero teased, holding my door open for me. He helped me out of the car with a laugh, and I swiped my face to make sure I didn't have any drool anywhere.

"I don't slob!"

"Yo' lyin' ass definitely slob. I be having to use a water-resistant pillowcase every time you sleep over here!" He was cracking the fuck up at his own joke until he noticed the pout on my face and pulled me to his side as he walked up the steps. "It's okay, bae, I love yo' lil' wet-mouth ass though."

I tried to shove him away, but his firm body barely moved. His grip on my waist tightened as he let us into the house and dropped my bag so he could wrap both arms around me. My ass was pretending to be mad, but his wet kisses on my neck quickly had me moaning and pressing into him. He was already trying to strip me out of my uniform, but I pulled away.

"Dinero, I need to take a shower first," I whined, making him immediately stop, and he looked up at me with a mischievous grin.

"Bet, come on." Grabbing my hand, he dragged me up the stairs and into the bathroom. Washing each other turned into him fucking me against the shower wall until we both erupted. After I came down from my post orgasmic bliss, we cleaned up and retired to his room. I slipped on one of his t-shirts to sleep in like I always did while he threw on some boxer briefs, and we climbed in bed. "So, did you think about it?" he asked in between kisses once we were under the covers, and I bit my lip in the dark. He was definitely serious and I took a minute to consider the pros and cons of actually agreeing. So far, Dinero was the most normal relationship that I'd ever had and while I was almost afraid of ruining things, I also didn't want to stop myself from getting the love I deserved.

"Yes," I damn near whispered as my heart pounded in my chest, waiting for his response. His body shifted so that he was sitting up on his elbow and looking down into my face, even though the only light in the room was coming through the window.

"Yeah what, you thought about it, or you movin' in?" his voice was anxious as he asked, and I smiled widely.

"Both," I barely got out before his lips were covering mine, and I realized I made the right decision.

CHAPTER FOURTEEN
CAMILLE

E ver since I'd gotten the confirmation that I was pregnant, I'd been getting hit with morning sickness that made my usually grumpy persona worse, and I hated that shit. It definitely wasn't helping sway my decision in the baby's favor, and most of the time I blamed that shit on Cash for impregnating me with his demon spawn. Even worse, I hadn't seen or heard from him since his goofy ass had threatened me, and my feelings were honestly hurt. Despite how dangerous I knew he was, I didn't believe he would really hurt me if I did go through with an abortion, but for some reason I wanted him to know that I hadn't. Baby Lucifer had my feelings all over the place.

I looked at my phone to see if he'd responded to my last text telling him we needed to talk and, of course, his rude ass had left me on read. I kept telling myself it was a good thing he hadn't blocked me, because that meant he was open to having a conversation, but knowing he was getting my calls and texts but not responding was torture. Once again, a new symptom of being pregnant, because I was a City Girl and usually had no problem cutting a nigga off. I didn't let niggas play with my heart, but here I was letting my standards go just for Cash to shit on me as soon as I said something he didn't like.

"Girl, what the hell wrong with you?" my mama shrilled, and I realized my emotional ass had started crying while I sat at her table waiting on my plate. Lately, I'd been craving her cooking something serious, so when I spoke to her earlier and she mentioned the spaghetti and catfish she was cooking, I made my way over there. Knowing that I wasn't the child prone to crying had her touching my forehead with the back of her hand as she looked down at me in concern. I rolled my eyes through my tears and grabbed a napkin to clean my face.

"Nothing's wrong with me unless you count being pregnant with the devil's spawn," I huffed, and she immediately started laughing like I'd told the funniest joke in the world.

"I called it! Darnell! Darnell, run me my money. I told you she was pregnant!" she yelled for my daddy who was in the other room while I looked on horrified. I didn't know what was worse, her knowing and not saying shit or them betting on my uterus. When my daddy slinked his big ass in the kitchen with a dub in his hand and his face twisted up, I decided that them betting was the worst. He slammed the money in her hand, looking disgruntled as hell, and she happily stuffed it down into her bra. "Don't be a sore loser, boo, I told you not to bet against me!"

"Maaan, you don't have to gloat, Allani. This shit was a fluke, you know damn well Ca'Mahri was the one more likely to have a baby first!"

"Y'all don't never be up in here placing bets on me and my sister! Y'all childish as hell!" I looked between the two of them in disapproval, but they both seemed unbothered.

"Girl, shut up." My mama waved me off. "We made y'all, we can do what we want," was her only defense as she finished making my plate and sat it in front of me. The food instantly snatched my attention and I started stuffing my mouth after rolling my eyes at her.

"So, now do we get to meet the father? 'Cause I feel like we need to have a one on one." My dad had his chest puffed out, seemingly over the loss of his money. For some reason I couldn't bring myself to repeat to my parents what I'd been saying to everybody else, which was that I wasn't keeping this baby. Even though they were both irritating as hell, I didn't have the heart to ruin their excitement. Maybe I had already made the decision and just didn't want to admit it to myself, considering that I was quickly approaching the point where an abortion would be out of the question.

The fact that I hadn't spoken to Cash didn't stop me from lying to my daddy and telling him I would set something up for them to meet. Satisfied, he went back to his recliner to finish watching TV while my mama sat telling me stories about her pregnancies and giving me tips that she'd learned along the way.

By the time I left I was good and full, with a Tupperware bowl filled with some more food for later. When I climbed behind the wheel, I checked my phone to see that Cash still hadn't gotten back to me, pissing me right off. Instead of heading home like I was about to, I drove out to Winnekta, even though I didn't know if he was home or not. On the way I called Ms. Keshia and she was happy to locate her son for me. Surprisingly, he was at his house with Kash and had been there the whole day. If I had known it would've been that simple I would've got his mama on the case sooner.

The whole drive I was talking to myself about how fucked up he had me. If it wasn't for the fact that Kash was there, I would've fucked around and went across his shit as soon as I laid eyes on him, but I was going to try to keep my cool.

Since his mama knew I was coming she opened the gate for me, so I had the element of surprise. I pulled up to his house and pressed the doorbell, tapping my foot impatiently while I waited on him to answer. Kash could be heard through the door being his usual rambunctious self and aside from that, his truck was in the driveway, so I knew he hadn't left. It still took him a long ass time by my standards, but after I held the doorbell down he finally swung the door open with his face balled up. He was shirtless and barefoot in a pair of dark blue jeans that hung off his ass just enough for me to see the band of his Ethika boxers. Seeing how good he looked had me sucking my teeth, because I sort of expected him to be just as sick as me despite him ignoring me. I'd worked myself up so much that I didn't even care about the evil look he was giving me.

"What you doin' here, Camille?" he questioned like he was already tired of being in my presence. That chipped away at my hard exterior, but I played it off.

"I been callin' and textin' you so we could talk but you've been ignoring the fuck out of me, which is crazy considering how you showed yo' ass at my house!" I shifted my weight with a hand on my hip as I tried to keep from slapping him. He just looked down at me without saying anything before laughing bitterly.

"I thought you wanted me to leave you alone? You wanted me to let you kill my baby in peace, right?" He got in my face and tilted his head. "I just gave you what you wanted, shit." I shuddered from how close he was, realizing how much I missed his mean ass, and my emotions hit me hard. Before I could stop myself, tears were racing down my cheeks and I was doing a full blown ugly cry.

"I don't want that thoooough!" I bawled, and he instantly jerked back, looking at me in confusion. Wiping my face, I tried to get myself together even as more tears fell. "I'm just scared, okay! This shit is happening so fast! How do I know you'll still want me and this baby in seven months? Niggas always say things then do another. Look at how fast you left me alone after you said you wouldn't! Then this lil' monster been giving me hell since you been gone! I shouldn't be doin' this alone, but you won't even answer the phone when I call!" His expression softened, and he cupped my face with both hands, wiping my tears with his thumbs.

"You're keeping the baby?" he asked softly, and the glimmer of hope in his eyes had my vision blurring with emotion.

"Y-yeah!" I hiccupped with a nod, and he kissed me deeply, letting his tongue explore my mouth as he grabbed me up into a hug. It felt good as hell to be in his arms again, and I hated that I'd taken so long to follow my heart, but I damn sure planned to make up for it.

"Amille!" Kash came running out and grabbed our legs with his cute self, getting in on the hug too. "Daddy, can Amille stay the night, pweese?" he looked up at Cash and pleaded, even going so far as clasping his hands together.

"You wanna stay the night with me and this lil' nigga?" He smirked, while Kash nodded and bounced around. Touching my chin, I pretended to think on it for a second before agreeing.

"Sure, but I'm gone need you to grab my food out the car and no, you can't get none!" I hollered after Cash, who ran to the car as soon as he heard food. My mama had packed more than enough for me to share, but with the way my appetite was set up I would eat the whole thing by myself and not feel bad about it. That was some shit we were going to have to get used to together, because I fully intended on him being at my beck and call since I was keeping his little demon baby. Now it was just time to get our families together, but I knew with the way our parents acted they'd get along just fine.

After getting things straightened out with Cash shit was running a lot smoother for me. He didn't play when it came to me and his baby and I loved that, I just hoped he kept the same energy when I got fat. So far, he'd gone out of his way to appease all of the worries that I'd mentioned to him. He was already making an effort to spend more time with Kash before I even came back, but other than that, he'd assigned me a security detail since they were having street issues. Although the person that had robbed them had virtually disappeared, he was still taking precautions, even insisting that I stay at his house with the end goal being me moving in, but I was still on the fence about that. Even though I told him not to, the nigga added money to my account every week and had set up a separate one for the baby so that, in his words, "I knew he wasn't a bitch-ass nigga." It hadn't even been a month yet, but he'd made me feel more secure than anybody I'd ever been with and I trusted him completely, which was saying a lot for me.

"So, am I invited to this family dinner y'all havin'? 'Cause I'ma need to get my good clothes ready if I am," Noelle asked as we sat down for lunch. It was one of those rare occasions when we all got a break at the same time, and I was glad too because I could sample whatever they were eating if it was different from mine.

"Duh, bitch! You just as much family as anybody else," Ca'Mahri said as she picked the onions and carrots out of her salad. Besides her digging her fingers all in that shit, I didn't have a taste for salad so I was already looking at what Noelle had.

"Periodt! Make sure Cash and Dinero invite somebody for me. I know them niggas got a cousin or uncle they can put me on with to make up for Russ's lame ass. Dang, greedy ass heffa!" she shrieked when I grabbed a handful of the fries that came with her burger.

"The only dude I see around like that is Snoop, but I'm sure he's gonna be there." I ignored her outburst and stuffed my mouth as she turned her nose up at the mention of Snoop. Since they'd first met they had been at odds, so she definitely didn't want to get hooked up with him and vice versa.

"You tried it. Ca'Mahri, it's on you boo, 'cause yo' sister trippin'." I shrugged as she rolled her eyes over to my sister, because that bitch had the same connections as me so she was wasting her time.

"I'll see what I can do, boo," Ca'Mahri lied, and Noelle gave me a teasing smirk, even though the joke was going to be on her silly ass. I dug into my pizza while they talked about what she was going to wear to dinner. That shit was gone in minutes and I was already picking at their food again since they were eating so damn slow.

"Hey Cami! Hey! What are you doing? Get your hands off me!" Turning around, I damn near choked seeing my bodyguard Lou strong arming Reyna. The look on her face was one of shock and then frustration when he didn't immediately let her past. As bad as I wanted to continue seeing her discomfort, I called him off, and she looked him up and down before taking a couple steps to our table.

"Camille, who is this and why is he handling your supervisor like a common criminal?" Straightening her clothes, she stood over me waiting on an answer. I tried to keep a straight face but it was hard, especially with Ca'Mahri and Noelle's ignorant asses giggling behind me.

"Oh, that's Lou, he's, ummm, my bodyguard."

"Bodyguard? You can't have a bodyguard, not here at work! It's unprofessional! Especially when he's physically assaulting staff!"

"Actually, it's nothing in the employee handbook about security and as long as he's not violating patients' rights then he's perfectly ok to be here, but in his defense you did walk up a little aggressively. I'd announce myself next time if I was you." I looked up at her with an innocent smile, pissing her off even more.

"We gone see about that!" She stormed off to go tell one of the higher ups, but I wasn't worried. I'd read the employee handbook so I already knew there was nothing in there about this type of situation, so the bitch was seriously reaching.

"You know you bouta fuck around and get fired," Noelle joked, and I shrugged, eating more of her fries. I wasn't afraid of Reyna, especially with my bank account sitting pretty the way it was. I was feeling like Rochelle from *Everybody Hates Chris*, my man had two jobs! We finished lunch and went back to work, and she never came back, like I knew she wouldn't. Fucking around with Cash had me even more outspoken than usual and I was loving it.

CHAPTER FIFTEEN
CASH

Finding Lox was proving to be much harder than I thought, and the fact that he hadn't made any other moves was unsettling as fuck. I was doing everything in my power to track him down though. I'd given Camille a bodyguard so when she wasn't with me I knew she'd be okay, and even my pops and Dinero had beefed up their security.

I was starting to get frustrated that not even a bounty had lured them niggas out, but it really wasn't much I could do. My plate was already full and I couldn't add searching the streets to my list of things I did in a day.

"Hey boss, Juelz is here," our receptionist stuck her head in my office door to let me know, and I clenched my jaw at the fact that she'd opened it without knocking. She had that shit bad, and even though I mentioned it before she still did it. I was beginning to think she did the shit on purpose just to piss me off. Shrugging off that petty shit, I made my way outside where Juelz was waiting and watching them load up the cars.

"What's up, Cash?" he greeted me once I made it to where he was standing.

"Sup Juelz?" His ass had less jokes and had straightened up since I started taxing him for coming late. Now he didn't play and was always on time so he could save himself an extra ten thousand per key.

The drop went off without a hitch and he was on his way, while my people put the money in my car. I was supposed to be meeting up with Dinero later so we could count it like always. In the meantime, though, I was going to stop and check up on my baby mama. Even though she had Lou with her I still wanted to see how she was doing and if she needed anything. I was trying to get her to follow her sister's lead and move in with me, but she was fighting me on that shit like she always did. I learned, though, that if I wanted her to do something I wanted then I needed to make her think it was her decision. It was going to take me a minute, but I was going to figure out a way to do just that.

She was off and had decided to keep Kash at her apartment with her, so I stopped through Harold's and grabbed us some chicken meals. I was hoping the eight piece and a pizza puff would get me some quick head, since all she cared about was food lately. I could already tell shorty was going to be a butter-ball with the amount of shit she ate every day, but if she wanted it she was going to get it.

I made it to her apartment and instantly greeted Lou, who let me in. He was standing just in the doorway, so I dapped him up as I passed. Setting the food down on the coffee table, I headed to the back to find Kash and Camille in the bed, and he was asleep on her growing titties like his little ass belonged there. I instantly entered and tried to move him, only for her to wave me off. When I told her I had some food out there for her she hurried to ease him onto the bed beside her. I knew that shit was going to get her ass.

"Did you get Lou somethin' too?" she asked as I walked behind her with my hands around her waist.

"Maaan, that big ass nigga don't need shit!"

"Cash," she stopped walking and whined. "That's not nice. Now I'ma have to order him something or cook—"

"I wish the fuck you would be in there tryna cook for another nigga!" I instantly grew jealous even though I knew she wasn't thinking about Lou in that way. "I already got him somethin' anyway, so you just go sit yo' greedy ass down and eat so I can slide up in there before I go." My fingers dipped into the front of her jeans, and she shuddered. Camille was always ready to go and the shit had me wanting to be inside her all the time. I'd forgot how good and wet pregnant pussy was until I started back fucking with her. She was already leaking as soon as I came in contact with her clit, and I quickly took a detour and led her into the bathroom.

"Caaaash, my food gone get cold!"

"I'ma be quick," I lied as she pouted, but still allowed me to help her out of her jeans. Dropping my slacks, I lifted her onto the bathroom sink and slid into her with ease.

"Mmmm," she let out a satisfied whimper, and I had to bury my face in her neck to keep from doing the same. Lifting her leg into the crook of my arm, I slowly drilled into her sopping wet center.

"Shit bae, why the fuck yo' pussy so damn juicy," I groaned, pushing myself deeper as she matched my strokes. With her damn near pressed into the mirror, I leaned back so I could watch as my dick grew more and more saturated with her creamy pussy juices.

"Baaaaby, mmm!"

"Fuck! Play with yo' clit, shorty." I bit into my lip as her fingers found her nub and rubbed frantically, drawing me closer to the edge. "Mmmm, let me taste that shit." Doing as I said, she slid her fingers into my mouth and I quickly wrapped my tongue around them, sucking hard like I did whenever I had her clit in my mouth.

"Oooh, fuck, I'm bouta come, Cash, shit!"

"Yeah? Come on yo' dick then, bae, I'm right behind you." I'd barely got the words out and she was jerking as an orgasm ripped through and a second later, I was filling her up with my seeds. Panting, we clung to each other, trying to get our beating hearts to slow down, and we cracked up laughing. "You a freak, bae, it don't make no sense how horny yo' lil' ass be."

"Don't play, you be just as ready as I do." She playfully rolled her eyes and shoved me.

"If you knew how good this pussy felt you'd wanna be in it all the time too," I told her truthfully, pecking her lips. I helped her down off the sink and we quickly got cleaned up before coming out and eating our food. We didn't even get the bags open good before Kash's little ass was up ripping and running, but we managed to get him to sit down so he could eat too.

Once I finished over there I met Dinero so we could count up the money, but halfway through he got a call saying that they had a location on Walt. It turned out that this whole time, him and his baby mamas were staying in a raggedy motel on the North side and the reason couldn't nobody find their asses was because they never left that muthafucka. After we got the address, I loaded up two guns while Dinero tucked a sawed-off rifle, and we were on the way.

"You ready?" he asked as we sat in the car directly in front of that nigga's room door.

"Hell yeah, I just hope he as much of a bitch as I think and tells us his cousin's whereabouts." He reached for the handle, nodding, and I stepped out too. Outside the door we could clearly hear his bad ass kids over the music that was playing, which put me at ease that this wasn't a set up. Confident that we had caught up to the right person, I turned around and donkey kicked his door.

"What the fuck! Go get the door, B, it might finally be Lox's ass." There was a brief pause and then the door swung open, drifting a gust of stale ass air that smelled like ass and dirty diapers. I instantly covered my nose and pushed past the half-naked, nappy-headed hoe that had answered the door. As soon as Walt saw us he hopped out of bed and tried to make a run for it, but I snatched him back by the shirt before he could run up in the bathroom.

"Fuck you think you goin', nigga?"

I dragged him out of the room while Dinero held his baby mamas at gunpoint and threatened them not to mention anything about what happened. Low key, I wanted to snatch them too, with their unfit asses. I didn't know what they'd gone through, but not even us storming in the room with guns and dragging their daddy away had stolen the kids' attention from the TV. That shit was crazy to me, but it wasn't my problem. Dinero, on the other hand, slipped a knot into the hand of the one that opened the door, with his softhearted ass.

"They just got yo' goofy ass, nigga. Them hoes bouta run up a bag on you and not get them kids shit but a Happy Meal."

"Long as they keep our names out this shit I couldn't care less. Besides, she's the one who gave up their location," he said, pulling off while I held my gun to Walt's neck in the backseat. Just like I knew he would, he was copping pleas the whole drive, but that shit was going in one ear and out the other because I didn't hear his cousin's name come up. It got to the point that I had to knock his ass out because I was tired of him crying. Instead of taking him to the warehouse, we drove to the funeral home and strapped him to a gurney in the basement.

"Wake yo' bitch ass up, nigga!" I barked, smacking him so hard a print of my hand showed up on his cheek. His eyes shot open and he groaned in pain. "Where the fuck yo' cousin at?"

"Ca-Cash, man, I don't know where that nigga at! He left me in that room and ain't been back since. Nigga wouldn't even take me to Milwaukee with him!" I believed his stupid ass, but still shared a look with Dinero like I was waiting on his opinion. "I'm for real! He left with his new bitch and didn't even give me a cut! I—"

Before I knew what was happening that nigga's head exploded, and I jumped back as his thoughts splattered against the wall. "Nigga, what the fuck? Why you do that?" I asked Dinero with my face balled up.

"He didn't know shit, it's obvious Lox just used his dumb ass. I'm surprised he ain't kill him himself." He set his gun on the table next to us and sighed. "Come on, let's get this nigga in here so I can go home to my girl."

"Ahhh, look at yo' soft ass! Don't nobody care that you tricked Ca'Mahri into movin' in with you," I teased, but I was proud of my big brother. He'd found himself a good girl and was taking shit to the next level.

He tried not to, but a smile was already tugging at his lips as we pushed the gurney over to the cremation chamber. "You just mad that Camille's pregnant ass ain't moved in yo' shit yet."

"Man, fuck you, she gone move or I'm gone move her!" I told him, dead serious. I had tried to give her time, but it was obvious she needed a little push. Running back and forth was getting played anyway, and soon she was going to be too big for me to be leaving her alone, even with Lou.

"Camille ain't going for that shit."

"Camille gone do whatever I tell her greedy ass, watch." I was sounding confident as hell, but I was going to have to figure out a way to get her to see my side of shit. We finished loading Walt's ass into the big ass oven and called the cleanup crew to handle the mess that Dinero made before leaving. The shit we'd just done was already forgotten and wasn't shit on my mind but digging in Camille's gushy pussy.

CHAPTER SIXTEEN
DINERO

I'd been running around all day grabbing shit for my mama and taking my grandma to the doctor, and I was tired as fuck. All the people moving around at the grocery store had both irritated and pissed me off, and if I could've paid somebody else to do that shit I would've, but my mama would've kicked my ass. She was the most traditional, privileged person I knew and if she could've got away with me and Cash mowing the grass on our property then she would, but that shit was way too big for us.

I helped my granny into the house and left her in front of the TV while I went back for the bags. Loading up both hands with as many bags as I could, I carried them inside and dropped them off in the kitchen just as my phone went off. I immediately recognized the number for Sandy Hills Rehabilitation Center and answered as worry froze me in my steps. They only ever called me once every few weeks to update me about what was going on with Tania, so to see their number gave me pause.

"Hello?"

"Hi, may I speak with Dinero Banks?" a crisp feminine voice asked and once I confirmed who I was, she continued. "Okay, well, I'm Nadine Smith, Tania's counselor, and she asked me to call you to come in for her next task. Would you be available later this week? Say, Friday at 11?"

"Oh yeah, I'll be there. Whatever Tania needs."

After giving me a few more details, Nadine ended the call and I looked up to see my pops leaned up against the wall, and just from the look on his face I knew he had something to say. Sighing, I shoved my phone in my pocket and prepared myself for the lecture of the day.

"How's Tania doin'?"

"She's good, getting better every day. They said she's doing well in her recovery and should be okay to come home soon." I was already smiling just thinking about it. Getting Tania back to her regular healthy self was important to me, and since I hadn't seen her since I dropped her off, I couldn't wait to lay eyes on her so I could physically see her progress.

"That's good to hear, but um, what are you going to be considering home, son? I know you're not movin' her in with you and Ca'Mahri? That's just asking for trouble." I honestly hadn't thought of that, I'd just been excited about her completing her treatment. My girl was understanding, though, so I didn't think she'd trip about me helping her out. Then again, though, she was understanding last time, but that didn't stop her from feeling some type of way.

"I mean, I could get her an apartment until she gets on her feet." I shrugged, and he looked at me like I had said the goofiest shit ever.

"Nigga, you tryna get a freshly recovered drug addict their own place right out of rehab?"

"Well, what do you think I should do then, Pops? She's gonna need some type of help—"

"She needs her family, Dinero," he said sternly. "I know you want to be the knight in shining armor, but I'm worried you're gonna fuck around and mess up what you got goin' on because of somebody you don't know anymore."

"I'm good, man, I'm not tryna blur the lines with Tania, and I'm definitely not tryna fuck up with Ca'Mahri. I'm just helping out a friend." I chuckled and his eyes narrowed in suspicion, but he threw his hands up in surrender.

"Ayite, don't say I didn't warn you." He walked off like he was Billy Dee or somebody, leaving me standing there thinking about what he'd said.

Friday came around faster than I thought it would and for some reason, I kept the meeting with Tania to myself, letting Ca'Mahri leave for work without mentioning that part of my day. My pops had me nervous as hell, to be honest, and worried that she'd spazz out on me or something. I left out like with her like I did every day except instead of heading into the city, I drove to the rehab.

Once I found a parking spot near the door, I was buzzed in and went straight to the front desk where a stale-faced Asian woman sat. "Um, I'm here for a meeting with Tania Cox and Nadine Smith," I stuttered, as she stared at me dryly.

"Okay, I need your ID and your signature on the sign-in sheet." She slammed a clipboard on the counter and I retrieved my identification from my wallet and slid it to her before quickly signing in. "You're good to go, it'll be the first office down that hall."

I followed her finger and mumbled a 'thank you' before heading to find Nadine. Just like she said, her name was on the door of the first office and I gave a light tap, twisting the knob once I was told to enter. This was going to be my first time seeing Tania since I dropped her off and a nigga was real-life nervous. I wasn't sure what to expect, but when I stepped inside the office I was completely blown away. Immediately, Tania jumped out of her seat and jumped into my arms. Right away I could see her glow was beginning to come back and she was filling out her clothes a lot better.

"Dinero! I missed you!" she squealed excitedly, giving me a tight squeeze. I hesitated to wrap my arms around her, but eventually did and hated how good it felt.

"I miss you too, T," I admitted and realized our hug had exceeded the amount of time a friend should embrace another when Nadine cleared her throat. We jumped apart like we'd been caught doing something we weren't supposed to as she came around her desk with her hand extended.

"Hi Dinero, I'm Nadine. It's nice to finally meet you."

"Likewise." I was talking to her and had even enclosed her hand in mine, but my eyes still shifted to a smiling Tania. It was hard to believe that she was the same girl I'd brought here, and I just couldn't stop looking at her. She looked just like she did back when we were younger and that shit had my head fucked up.

"Okay, okay, well have a seat," Nadine instructed before going back to her swivel chair as me and Tania took up the two spots in front of her desk. "We've called you here today, Dinero, because we've been having discussions about the people who mean the most to us. Your name came up, and Tania explained to me how instrumental you were to bringing her to this point, so I told her to write down the effects you've had on her wanting to get better."

I was already prepared to downplay my role because I felt like it was the least I could do, but Tania quickly put up a hand to stop me. "I know you don't want to take any credit for this,

Dinero, but if it wasn't for you there's no telling where I would've been. You've done more for me in a few months than my whole family has done my whole life, and that means so much to me because before I ran into you on the street I didn't feel like I deserved any help. I felt like God was punishing me for killing our baby, and I was ready to die, to be honest." She got choked up and Nadine hurried to hand her a box of Kleenex.

"Go ahead, Tania," she encouraged soothingly. Nodding, Tania wiped her face and gathered herself as she continued.

"I-I wanted to die that night, and then I ran into you and I felt like it had to be a sign, right? I mean what are the odds that I'd run into my high school sweetheart years later and thousands of miles from our home? Then when you helped me instead of immediately discarding me like everyone else had, I knew that God had sent you back to me because he wants me to live and I know when you brought me here I didn't show it, but I just want to thank you for everything you've done for me." By now even Nadine's eyes were glistening from the passionate way she spoke, and I had to admit that she hit a nigga's heart. She reached over the arm of the chair and hugged my neck, leaking all types of tears and snot on my damn shirt, as I held her to me and allowed her to get it all out.

"I got you, T, and I'm glad that I was able to be there when you needed me. You my people so I'm gone always look out for you no matter what," I promised, meaning every word. Hearing the way she felt about my coming back into her life at the time I did made it all worth it, and I felt good as fuck that I'd been able to help her when no one else had.

The meeting went well after that and I listened to the progress she'd made before she took me around so we could do a few of the activities they had. The shit was really like a glorified spa and had everything from tennis to basketball and a damn buffet style cafeteria. Real shit, as much as I was spending for her to be there I was glad that she was getting all of the benefits that she could out of the program. She was doing well, though, and was going to be eligible for the outpatient programs in a few weeks, which didn't give me very much time to figure out her living situation.

Once we said our goodbyes, I went about the rest of my day handling business as usual. I had a few pick-ups to do and after I had all the money accounted for and put away, I stopped by to grab some food from Gibsons before heading home. Ca'Mahri was already home when I got there and greeted me with open arms.

"Hey baby." She cheesed, and I lifted her up with one arm, covering her lips with mine.

"What yo' fine ass been doin'?" I asked between pecks as I carried her further inside and set our food on the kitchen island. She'd been living with me for almost a month now and it was just as lit as I thought it'd be. Not only did I have in-house pussy but she was good ass company. Ca'Mahri had me doing all the lame ass couple shit that females loved and niggas denied enjoying, like movies and game nights. We even had shows and shit that we wouldn't watch without each other.

"Nothin'. Just talkin' to my sister and Noelle and missin' you." She stroked the back of my neck thoughtfully as I put her on the island and stood between her silky legs. The pajama shorts she was wearing bunched around her thighs, snatching my attention, and instantly drew my hands there.

"Oh yeah?"

"Yep, what you do all day?" The question was innocent enough, but I still stiffened as my time with Tania came to mind. Omitting that I'd visited her was one thing, but straight lying and leaving out that I took my ass up there was something totally different. That's exactly what the fuck I did though. Burying my face in her neck, I dropped a few kisses there and told her about everything I'd done, leaving out Tania entirely as I let my hand slip inside her shorts. Within minutes I had her bent over and holding on to the island for dear life as I fucked her deeply from the back. By the time we both climaxed and cleaned up to eat we were on to different topics, like Camille's pregnancy and who we were going to hook Noelle up with for the family dinner we were throwing, and a nigga could breathe a little easier. I knew eventually, though, I was going to have to break down and tell her that Tania was being released soon and would need me to look out for her. I damn sure couldn't leave her high and dry after the things she'd told me, but I'd also need to find a way to help and keep a close eye on her. Shit was crazy, but I was sure I could handle it just like I did everything else.

CHAPTER SEVENTEEN

CA'MAHRI

I t was finally the night to bring our families together and I was excited as hell. Dinero's parents had a lot in common with me and Camille's so I knew they'd get along good, at least I hoped so anyway. The last thing we needed was for them to not like each other after our relationships had come so far. Shit, I was already shacking up with Dinero and Camille was pregnant and showing, so it would definitely be awkward as hell going forward.

I moved around our bedroom singing Jasmine Sullivan's song "BPW," right along with her as I added the final touches to my look. We'd decided at the last minute that we would have a barbeque instead of a stuffy ass dinner, and that way things would be more social, especially with the added guests. The weather was perfect, at seventy degrees with the sun shining and an occasional breeze that would keep us from getting too hot in the backyard. I had on a cute, yellow sundress that looked good against my chocolate skin, and a pair of matching wedges that strapped up my ankles. My hair was piled up on top of my head in a messy bun with my baby hairs slicked, and I kept my jewelry to minimum, only wearing a pair of small gold hoops, a layered necklace, and my gold watch.

"And even though weeeee aiiin't official you know I ain't no regular girl!" I sang off key as I sprayed on my perfume.

"Yo' ass up here havin' a concert and I'm hungry, bae, come on." Dinero eased behind me and rested his chin on my shoulder with an exaggerated pout. He was wearing a white t-shirt with a yellow and blue block of color across the chest, and some dark blue shorts. He'd matched it with a pair of white Gucci sneakers that were crispy as hell so I knew he'd just bought them, probably only for the day's events. As usual, he wasn't flashy with his jewelry, only wearing his Patek, a couple of chains, and a stud in one ear. If it wasn't for the fact that he was already tripping about how long I was taking, I would've tried to get a quickie in, but there was plenty of time for that.

"I'm done." I giggled, swaying with him as the song came to an end and another started to play.

"Ayite, you better stop grindin' on me before our people hear yo' ass screamin' like a cat in heat!" He gave me that look and I instantly moved away from him. I wasn't trying to have my business out there and considering how vocal Dinero always had me, it would be, considering that we were hosting. I'd already heard his parents and Ms. Dorothea arrive a little bit ago, and I knew Cash, Camille, and my parents would be coming soon too.

"Ok, let's go then." I disconnected my phone from the Bluetooth speaker and grabbed his hand so we could go downstairs. This barbeque was going to be completely handled by us, so I'd made a couple of side dishes and so had Camille, Ms. Keshia, and Ms. Dorothea, even though we'd told her she didn't have to. After cursing us all the fuck out, she told us she going to cook the greens and spaghetti since she didn't know if she could trust any of ours. That little old lady was something else and I always found myself either dying laughing or extremely shocked when she was around.

As soon as we descended the stairs, Cash, Camille, and little Kash were entering looking so cute I wanted to take a picture. She had on a tight-fitting, pink and white dress that showed off her little pudge and some pink sandals, while the guys both wore white Champion tees and gray shorts, with white Air Force Ones. They looked like a little family already, and I quickly gave them all a hug before Kash could run off.

"Where you want this?" Cash asked, holding up the two pans he had covered by aluminum foil.

"Just take it to the kitchen, that's where everything is." Dinero and him walked off while I talked to my sister. "You nervous?" I spoke once we were alone.

"Hell no, as ghetto as these folks are they're gonna get along just fine. Daddy don't be doin' too much." Shrugging, she tossed her hair over her shoulder as the door opened up, bumping her back.

"The party's here!" Noelle came in shouting, with her crazy self. She looked good in a black t-shirt dress and platform Chuck Taylor's. Since her ass couldn't cook she had a bunch of chips in her arms with a bottle of Casamigos tucked in there.

"Hey boo! You look cute!" I complimented, and this fool turned to the side and struck a pose.

"Thank you, y'all look good too. Now where the niggas at?"

Laughing, I shrugged my shoulders while Camille rolled her eyes. "Nobody's here yet, hot coochie! You gone have to wait a little bit for people to arrive. In the meantime, you can take that into the kitchen," I directed, and she switched off sucking her teeth.

"That bitch crazy." We chuckled as we headed in the same direction that everybody else had gone. There was food on almost every surface in the kitchen and I knew we'd be having to send people away with foil pans full of food just to get rid of some. Everybody was already in the backyard except for Ms. Dorothea, who was warming up different dishes for when the meat was done. I could already smell it and it had my stomach growling hard as fuck.

"Come on in here and feed my great-gran, girl, I done already stole a few pieces of meat and made you a plate," she fussed at the sight of Camille, and I laughed at how fast her greedy ass took a seat and began to dig into the plate. "Ca'Mahri, don't just stand there and look pretty, baby, take this pan out to Kendrick and tell him not to burn these hot dogs or I'ma get in his ass!" Now it was my sister's turn to crack up as I was put straight to work while she got to sit and eat. I lifted up the heavy ass pan of seasoned chicken and carried it out of the open patio doors right to where Dinero's daddy stood over the smoking grill. He was busy filling the pan next to him with the finished meat when I walked up. We were about to switch when Dinero popped up and lifted it for me with a smirk.

"I got you, baby," he said, and I leaned up for a quick kiss.

"Aye, don't smush that meat tryna be all lovey dovey!" Ms. Keshia called from under the umbrella table we had set up, and my cheeks flushed, but Dinero wasn't fazed at all. He pecked me again before walking off and slapping my ass as he did. His ass thought he was slick, but I knew he'd probably only took that pan in the house so he could pick in it.

"Baby, cut that up! You know that's my shit!" Mr. Kendrick called out to his wife, and she quickly did, filling the entire backyard with the sounds of Keith Sweat's song "Nobody."

"Aww, here y'all ass go!" Cash grunted from his spot next to his mama and turned up the beer he was holding. It was obvious he was embarrassed by their displays of affection as she sang the girl parts and he whined like Keith Sweat. I didn't care what he said, I thought they were hilarious. I stayed for the show, throwing in an occasional adlib and acting as their background singer.

"Now you know you bogus as hell for egging them on." Dinero came and pulled me into his lap under the umbrella, and I shrugged.

"Y'all some haters, they're cute." By now the couple was swaying together in front of the grill, unbothered by their children's heckling. "You think that's what we're gonna be like?" I asked softly, shifting so I could look down into his face.

"You wanna be some old freaks, going around and embarrassing our kids and shit?" He lifted his eyebrows in amusement, and I nodded with a smirk. "Yeah, that do sound about right." Laughing, he squeezed me to him and gave me a kiss just as the doorbell sounded throughout the house. We were all in the backyard now, waiting on Kendrick to finish the last batch of meat, and some of Cash and Dinero's crew had arrived, so I knew it had to be my parents and I jumped up, pulling Dinero along with me.

"Ma! Daddy!" I released Dinero's hand and gave each of my parents a hug, before pulling them inside. "Dinero, these are my parents, Allani and Darnell. Parents, this is my boyfriend, Dinero," I gushed as my daddy shook his hand and he gave my mama a kiss on the cheek and a warm hug. Of course, my daddy ended up holding Dinero back a bit while I led my mama toward the back. Her head was on the swivel taking in every detail of the beautiful mansion and complimenting us.

"Oooh, honey! When you said he was doing well you didn't say *this* well! You done got you a very successful man, girl, yassss!" We chuckled and she gave me a five on the sly. My mama stayed trying to be cool, which was why she had come dressed like one of the Real Housewives of Atlanta in some black jean shorts that hugged her figure and a white camisole with a patterned, kimono-type shawl. Her ass even wore some heels like this wasn't a regular barbeque. Looking at us, nobody would guess she was my mama and not my older sister, despite the few grays that were sprinkled throughout her pressed hair.

I took a peek back at Dinero and my daddy and they seemed to be getting along just fine as they talked about his luxury car lot, like my daddy was really in the market for a damn sports car. As long as they were laughing, though, I didn't even care.

"Y'all, look who finally made it!" I announced once we reached the patio doors, and everybody's head turned in our direction.

"Oh, hell naw!" Ms. Keshia huffed, and I felt my mama's body stiffen as they stared each other down. "I just know damn well that ain't Allani Pine!" she called my mama by her maiden name, and I was stuck looking between the two. Even Camille, who had gotten up to come greet our mama, was frozen in place until both ladies' faces split into wide grins and they ran across the yard to each other like they were on *The Color Purple*.

"I missed you so much, girl! I thought you had left!"

"We did for a lil' bit, but you know I'm Wild Hundreds 'til the day I die!" They laughed and hugged again as me and Camille shared a look. "Y'all, this was my best friend in high school! What are the fuckin' odds that our kids ended up fuckin' around?"

My mama waved us over and filled us all in on how they used to spend all of their time together. She even knew Kendrick, but since she hadn't met my daddy until a year after they all separated, he was new to the bunch. That didn't stop him from blending right in and before we knew it, we were all sitting around the table laughing.

My mama and Ms. Keshia eventually started talking about getting together to plan Camille a gender reveal and baby shower, while our dads talked about the trucking business and investments. I was good and tipsy sitting in Dinero's lap, and singing some of the songs that were playing.

"Let's go in the house real quick," he said so low that nobody else could hear, and shifted so I could feel his hardness against my ass. Giggling, I shook my head because I wasn't falling for that shit. He'd already threatened me earlier and I was not about to be shouting while my daddy was there.

"Noooo, everybody's gonna notice if we both disappear."

"Not if you go first and then I come in a little after." His eyebrows lifted, awaiting my answer, and after looking around to see that nobody was paying us any attention, I quickly agreed. "Ayite, gone head, bae. I'ma meet you in the down-stairs bathroom in like two minutes. Have all this shit off," he ordered, and I bit into my lip, before giving him a quick kiss.

"Okay, hurry up!" Discreetly looking around one more time, I ducked inside and was about to grab some of the cake on the island, when I saw Ms. Dorothea sprawled out on the floor with blood coming out of her head.

CHAPTER EIGHTEEN
CAMILLE

The music was so loud that it took us all a minute to hear my sister inside screaming, but when we did, we took off running. It was something about it that let us all know something was wrong and when we entered the kitchen and saw her administering CPR to Ms. Dorothea, I sprang into action. Being in the medical field had us equipped to deal with this to a degree, but the fact that it was a family member made it hard not to panic.

After calling an ambulance, I tried to keep Cash and his family back while my mama and sister worked on her until they arrived. It was pure pandemonium, and the six minutes that it took for help to arrive felt like forever. Kendrick insisted on riding in the ambulance with his mama while everybody else grabbed their keys so they could drive.

"Baby, I'll stay here with Kash, you go make sure Ms. Dorothea's okay."

"Naw Camille, I need you there with me. Please, shorty!" The look of pain on his face had me agreeing, even though I knew the hospital was no place for Kash at the moment.

"Okay, okay, let's go." Since Kash was worn out from playing in the sun and eating all day, his daddy carried him out to the car and was barely able to get him strapped in his seat, so I took over. "Just go ahead, I got him!" I waved Cash away as I hopped in the backseat and quickly buckled him in.

It was like a car show the way everybody sped out of their gates. I sat in the back praying the whole way because Cash and Dinero were both eating the highway up, and a trip that should've taken fifteen minutes was shaved down to five. When he finally pulled up to the hospital I was almost too scared to get out because my legs felt like jello, and I was sure that I'd probably let a little bit of pee out.

After I finally got my bodily functions back, I caught up with Cash, who had the baby tucked under his arm like a sack of potatoes and was bumrushing through the emergency room doors. Ca'Mahri, Dinero, Ms. Keshia, and our parents were all in the waiting room looking completely distraught. Even with me not being a blood relative I could understand their pain because I'd grown to love Ms. Dorothea like my own grandma.

Kendrick came out of the back a short time later cursing out the nurses, and Ms. Keshia had to pull him away from the emergency entrance so they wouldn't call the police. He'd sit down for a little bit, but he and his sons took turns going to the nurse's station and harassing the lady at the front desk until it got to the point that Ms. Keshia told them she'd be the one asking for updates.

I sat next to Cash, rubbing his back as he held his head in his hands. They'd all somewhat calmed down and were silently hoping for the best. Kash was laid across my lap knocked out and drooling all down my leg, but he was completely unaware of the shit going on and I was glad for that. His little bad ass loved Dorothea and when he wasn't running around causing havoc, he was sitting up under her and eating all of the snacks she kept in her room for him.

"Baby, why don't you take Kash home and get some rest. I know you wanna be here, but I can already see your eyes drooping," Ms. Keshia finally said to me after a few hours had passed and we still hadn't gotten any news.

"Yeah, gon' home, shorty. Y'all don't need to be sitting in these uncomfortable ass chairs all night." Cash looked up and surprisingly agreed with his mama. I thought for sure he'd want me to stay, and even though I was dog tired, I didn't want to leave him. He quickly noticed my reluctance and grabbed my face, giving me a couple pecks on my lips. "It's cool, bae, you and my babies need to go home and rest. I'll call you if we find out anything," he promised, already lifting Kash off of my lap and standing to his feet. I stopped to hug everybody and let them know I was taking the baby home for the night, before taking his hand and walking out to the car. He strapped Kash back into his seat and pressed a kiss to the side of his head before shutting the door. For a second I thought he was going to drive us, until he dropped his keys in my hands and hugged me tightly, then dropped to kiss my belly.

"Be safe, okay? Call me when you make it in."

"Okay, I love you, Cash." It was the first time I'd said it and I definitely didn't want it to be under these circumstances, but I needed him to know.

"I love you too, shorty." He forced a smile, helping me into the car and waiting while I pulled off. We'd left so fast that Lou had to drive behind us, and he'd been sitting in the parking lot the whole time, but when I drove off, he was right behind me. As soon as I was alone my ass was sobbing hysterically, to the point that I almost couldn't see. My emotions washed over me hard and fast just thinking about the last conversation I'd had with her in the kitchen.

*"Girl, you better slow down, that plate ain't goin' nowhere!"
Ms. Dorothea looked up from the oven and laughed at the way I was
scarfing down my plate. She'd hooked me up with collards, baked
macaroni, sweet potatoes, two brats, a chicken leg, and a cold Pepsi,
and I'd already swallowed down half.*

*"Tell your great-gran that, 'cause it's like she takes all my food
so I'm always hungry," I complained, taking a bite of my last brat,
only making her laugh harder. She put another two pans of food
into the oven and came to sit down next to me with a smile on her
face.*

*"Well, you gone have to get used to that, baby. The Banks breed
big babies! I remember when I had Kendrick, that boy was damn
near twelve pounds, and so were Dinero and Cash! Shit, I think even
lil' Money was about ten pounds, tore Vernique lil' ass right up!"
She nodded with a smile while my eyes damn near popped out of my
head, choking as I tried to recover from my food going down the
wrong pipe.*

*"Twelve pounds!" I managed to croak out, and she started
laughing again before giving me a firm pat on the back.*

*"You'll be fine, I know a few tricks that'll make sure that baby
slide right out. Cash acted like he was ashamed of Vernique, so he
didn't bring her around until she had already had lil' Money, and I
don't blame him 'cause I'd be shamed to admit that I skeeted in that
thang too," she rolled her eyes and said. "But you, I can tell my Cash
loves you."*

*I was already shaking my head and ready to disagree, but she
held up a hand to stop me. "Don't be so sure. Men show you
before they tell you, and I see it all in the way he handles you.
That boy is in love! And I'm happy about it. You and your sister
came right in the nick of time to take care of my boys, because
they need y'all. I been sticking around just waiting on them to
find the right women to settle down with. I can already tell y'all
gone take good care of them," she repeated, and fear instantly*

gripped my chest as I read between the lines of what she was saying.

"Oh no, Ms. Dorothea, don't talk like that. You're gonna be around to help me take care of this baby you done jinxed me with!" I tried to break the tension with a joke, and she looked at me like I was crazy as hell.

"Girl, what the hell you talkin' 'bout? I wasn't saying I was gone die, child. Shit, I know I ain't goin' nowhere for a while, I'm too stubborn! I was talkin' about livin' my best life, hell. All my kids are raised, girl, I'm ready to do me!"

Just thinking about that had me laughing through my tears. Ms. Dorothea was a whole character, and I just knew she was going to pull through this. Like she'd said, she was way too stubborn to die anytime soon. I kept that thought in mind the rest of the drive until I was pulling up to the gate, and I quickly let myself in. It was going on one in the morning and regardless of the lights around their property, it was still a little too freakishly quiet out here. I squinted to make sure that Lou was still behind me and once I saw that he was, I pulled into the long drive and came to a stop in front of Cash's house.

"I got him." Lou came up behind me as I unstrapped Kash and took him from my arms once I was done. That was a relief because I didn't know if I'd be able to unlock the door while I was holding his little butt.

"Thanks." I sighed and led the way up the porch. Once I had the door open, he eased Kash back into my arms and I ducked inside, getting ready to shut the door, but he stopped me.

"Try to get some sleep, I'm sure Ms. Dorothea is gonna be just fine. Lock u—"

The rest of what he was saying was cut off as his brains splashed out of his head and I screamed, seeing a dark figure step over where his body fell. I backed up as they advanced on me and I tried to find something that I could use to defend myself, which was hard considering that I still had Kash in my arms. Rushing me, he sent a hard fist into my face, and I saw stars before everything went black.

CHAPTER NINETEEN
VERNIQUE

"What the fuck are you doin'? That bitch was holdin' my baby!" I fussed, immediately rushing over to Kash, who was now awake and crying. Picking him up, I rocked him trying to get him to calm down, but he wasn't having it and I completely blamed his stupid ass daddy for the disconnect. After I got back from vacation he'd made it almost impossible to see my baby and then had the nerve to have his mama doing visits like she was DCFS. Then, after his pit bull attacked me in front of our son, he really cut down, like I was somehow at fault. It was ridiculous. All of this was because I wanted a break. I deserved a break after being a single parent since Kash was born. It was me going to doctor appointments and staying up with a sick baby. It was me potty training and cleaning his pissy draws and bed when he had an accident. I was the one that took him to the park and put him to bed, but Cash was allowed to come and go as he pleased. All he did was give me money and when he did get our baby, most of the time he was with Ms. Keshia.

So, yes, I felt like a vacation was long overdue and when my girl asked me to come for free, I jumped at the chance. I didn't understand why he was so upset when he'd agreed to keep Kash. It wasn't like I just dropped him off and didn't say shit, so I didn't get the issue or why it had to result in him basically kidnapping my son. Then he went from being a hoe to settling down with some random bitch in the time that I was gone. To be honest, I didn't know what pissed me off more, but it didn't help that the bitch put her hands on me.

I finally got Kash to calm down enough that he was merely whimpering, so I hurried to get him out to the car, dodging the huge corpse on my way out. I knew that they'd all be at the hospital with Dorothea's old ass after my cousin that worked at the hospital called me asking why I wasn't there. Hating ass bitch was thirsty to tell me that Cash's whole family was there including his bitch, so I drove there ready to act a fool. I didn't give a fuck about his grandma being on her deathbed. When I got there, though, Camille was leaving and it just made more sense to follow her since she had my son. As soon as I saw her heading back to Cash's house, I took a shortcut and managed to beat her there by two minutes. The shit worked out almost too perfectly, and now I was ready to get the fuck out of dodge.

Since I didn't have a car seat with me, I sat him down and tightened the seat belt around him just in case he got to wiggling. By the time I dropped into the passenger seat, my partner in crime was back. He sped out of the gate so damn fast that I clicked my seat belt, which was something I usually didn't do. I understood the rush because once my baby daddy found out what I did, he was going to go on a rampage, but I just wanted to spend some time with my baby for a couple of days. He'd probably still be pissed about the dead body and his girlfriend getting hit, but in my opinion that was just my lick back since he didn't do shit about her giving me a black eye.

"Ayite Lox, slow yo' ass down! My baby's not even strapped

in right!" I shouted once I felt like we were a safe distance away, but his foot never eased off the pedal. "Did you hear me?"

"Shut up, damn! Yo' ass don't never be quiet!" I jerked back at his snappy tone because it wasn't something I was used to. Since I'd met him in Cancun, he had been nothing short of a gentleman, buying me anything I wanted and going above and beyond for me. Having a nigga that was fine, paid, and not afraid to share was the ultimate goal. Shit, he was even the one that had suggested I take my son back and promised to help, after I filled him in on the way Cash was treating me. Folding my arms, I turned to the window with an attitude, thinking that he was going to apologize, but he just cut the radio up loudly and continued to drive. Once we got to the Air BnB he was staying at out North, I reached for the handle and instantly froze when I felt him pressing a gun to my head.

"I'ma need you to call yo' baby daddy," he demanded, making my face scrunch in confusion.

"What?" My voice shook and I stilled, too scared to even turn around at this point. His ass had been acting crazy as hell the whole night, but after the way he'd killed the bodyguard, I didn't know what he was capable of. My question had him shoving my head roughly with the gun's barrel as he repeated himself.

"Call. Cash."

"You know he's not gonna answer for me, especially with his grandma in the hospital. I—"

"Call that nigga mama then. You said y'all was cool, right? She'll answer," he cut me off, and as bad as I wanted to ask him why, I knew better when he'd gone so far as to pull a gun on me.

"Okay, but can you at least take the gun off me?" I asked shakily, and he scoffed.

"Naw, not until you get Cash on the phone."

A flurry of questions ran through my mind as I tried to figure out on my own what he was doing. Did he work for Cash? Was he trying to get in good with him by dry snitching? My fingers shook as I called Ms. Keshia's phone, and it took two tries for her to finally answer, but when she did I breathed a sigh of relief. Hopefully he wouldn't shoot me since I did what he wanted.

"Put it on speaker!" Lox whispered so she wouldn't hear, and I hurriedly did what he said, making her voice fill the car.

"Hey, um, I'm gonna have to call you back, V, we're dealing with a family emergency right now."

"Wait! Ms. Keshia, I actually really need to talk to Cash and he's not answering his phone. Please, it's an emergency, it's got to do with his girlfriend." I thought quick on my feet, knowing that he'd probably come running if it had anything to do with that bitch.

"What about Camille?" Her voiced raised an octave and I rolled my eyes, but resisted the urge to smack my lips. Ms. Keshia hadn't ever been particularly mean to me, but I knew damn well she'd never sound that concerned about me.

I tried to hide it, but I'm sure my attitude was evident in my voice when I said,

"It's personal, can I please just speak to Cash and if wants then he can just fill you in." I heard her mumbling under her breath like I was getting on her nerves, and then she was talking lowly to Cash. At the mention of his precious girlfriend, he got louder and immediately came on the line, making me bristle despite my current situation.

"Vernique, yo, I'm not in the mood for no bullshit right now, so this better be important!" he growled, and Lox's thirsty ass quickly snatched the phone away with a twisted grin.

"I'd say me havin' yo' son and yo' baby mama is pretty important."

CHAPTER TWENTY
CASH

I instantly hopped out of my chair and pulled my phone out to call Camille as anger coursed through me. Even if this was a joke, it was far from funny and just the implication that my son was in harm's way had me seeing red. I could give a fuck less about Vernique but my son, I'd go to war behind him.

"Oh, you wanna die, huh? Who the fuck is this?" I asked, growing more pissed when Camille still hadn't answered her phone. Switching gears, I dialed Lou and his shit just rang until the voicemail picked up.

"Awww, listen at baby Banks tryna sound tough. If you want yo' kid back you're gonna have to come out yo' pockets tho'. How much you think this lil' muhfucka worth, Nique? I'd say the heir to the Banks's throne is worth at least a half a quarter mil'. Matter fact, I shouldn't even shortchange myself like that. Let's just gone head and round that up to say, five hundred thousand. That's a nice number." This nigga had the nerve to laugh in my ear. I wanted so bad to tell his ass to suck

my dick, but the fact that I couldn't reach Camille or Lou told
me there was some truth to what he was saying. My pops and
Dinero were now huddled around me looking concerned, but I
was too focused on the bitch nigga in my ear.

"Ayite, but I need to know Kash is straight. Let me talk to
him, put him on the phone," I demanded, even though some of
the bass left my voice. My son was my heart and if anything
happened to him because of this street shit, then I'd be fucked
up. This was the shit Camille had been talking about, and I'd
been so confident that I had everything under control and now
some nigga had snatched up my son.

I heard him shuffling around a little before Kash's crying
became loud and prominent, and I pressed the phone harder to
my ear. Dude was definitely going to die for this stunt, but if he
hurt my son then I'd make sure to torture him first. "Aye, say
hey to yo' daddy."

"Daaaaddy!"

"Kash! Kash!" I called frantically.

"Ahhh, listen at you. *Kash! Kash!* You sound like a bitch!" he
laughed, and my jaw clenched tightly. I already couldn't wait
to kill this nigga. "Ayite look, I'ma call you back with a location
for you to bring my money. Stay by the phone!" The three
beeps let me know his bitch ass had hung up, and now everybody was surrounding me asking questions.

"I gotta go to the crib, somethin' might be wrong with
Camille." I was handing my mama her phone back and about
to leave, but Ca'Mahri jumped right in my way.

"What you mean something's wrong with my sister? What
happened to Camille!" she yelled, moving with me as I tried to
go around her.

"I don't know, I'm goin' to see now, Cam." I tried to keep
my voice calm so she wouldn't get any more worked up, but

that shit didn't help at all. Looking at Dinero, I motioned for him to help and he finally jumped into action, grabbing her shoulders and telling her to calm down.

"No! If my sister's in trouble then I'm goin' too!"

"Give me yo' keys, bro."

"What's goin' on, Cash? Where's Camille and my grandbaby!" Now both women were going off as Dinero fished out his keys and handed them off to me.

"Nah, y'all go check that shit out together, I got them," my pops ordered, snatching up both Ca'Mahri and our mama. Neither of them were a match for his buff ass, and it gave us time to leave. Since I still had the keys, I jumped in the driver's seat and pulled off while I filled Dinero in on what I knew.

"What the hell? This shit crazy, man." His face balled up once I finished. "You think this shit random? What if it's Lox weird ass? We still ain't found that nigga."

"How the hell Vernique know his ass though?" I didn't know what to think. We hadn't had any other issues out of Lox since he robbed the trap. Had his ass really just popped back up out of nowhere, and with my baby mama of all people? If Vernique had anything to do with this shit, she was going to die right along with that nigga, and I didn't give a fuck that she was Kash's mother. Hell, she didn't!

Dinero was still talking, but I wasn't paying his ass any attention as we pulled up at home and saw the gate sitting wide open. I could see up ahead where Lou's car sat with the brake lights glowing, and my heart pounded in my chest. This whole time I'd just been trying to get to Camille, but pulling up and seeing the scene before me filled me with dread. I was almost afraid to look, but I kept driving until I stopped in front of my house. The front door was wide open and I could clearly see Lou's big ass laid out right in front of it. There was really no point in even checking him because the pool of blood pouring out of his head let me know he was gone. I shared a look with Dinero and rushed inside, frantically searching for Camille. I saw her feet first and instantly my heart dropped as I ran over to her. The lights flicked on, so I was able to see, and I quickly inspected her body, not seeing any visible gunshots. She did, however, have a big ass knot on her forehead.

"Camille! Camille, baby, get up!" I lifted her body in my arms and grabbed her face, giving it a few light slaps.

"Hmm." Moaning, she came to and squinted as her eyes tried to adjust to the light. "Kash, where's Kash?" she questioned weakly, trying to sit up but fell back against me right as Dinero returned and shook his head, letting me know Kash really wasn't there.

"Fuck! Baby, I need to take you to the hospital. You might have a concussion." Camille was still looking confused as I lifted her in my arms bridal style and carried her to the car. My brother followed behind me and put in a call to the cleanup crew.

After I got Camille settled across the backseat, I climbed in with her and he drove us right back to the hospital. Shorty was crying the whole way and trying to explain what happened but aside from Lou getting killed and her being knocked out, she didn't know shit. She didn't even mention Vernique, just a nigga dressed in dark clothes.

"It's okay, bae, I got you now, but you can't tell these muhfuckas none of that. You gone have to tell them you tripped or some shit, but please do not tell them what you just told me." I stared down into her face to make sure she understood me. The last thing we needed was the police sniffing around and asking questions. I wanted full control over how this shit ended. She gave a slight nod as we pulled up to the hospital, and I carried her inside.

"Aye, I need some help over here, my girl pregnant and she's hurt!" That drew the attention of everybody in the emergency room, and they quickly came out with a stretcher. A nurse directed me to the waiting area as they wheeled her back, and my jaw clenched irritably. I didn't like that they didn't want to let me back for something as simple as a head injury when Camille was pregnant with my baby, but I wasn't going to trip. Instead, I made my way over to my family with my brother, and as soon as Ca'Mahri saw us she jumped up with questions.

"Where's Camille? What happened to my sister, Cash?" Sighing, I dropped into a chair and rested my head in my hands.

"She's in the back gettin' looked at. A muhfucka knocked her out, but other than that she's fine."

"Somebody did what! She ain't fine if somebody put their hands on her, she's pregnant!"

After all the shit I was dealing with, the last thing I was trying to do was listen to Ca'Mahri yelling. I could definitely understand her concern because if it was my brother I would've been ready to blow some shit up. Unfortunately, it wasn't just about Camille and the baby. My son was in danger and my fucking granny was fighting for her life. It was a lot going on, and all I wanted her ass to do was get out of my face so I could think.

"Bro, please. I ain't tryna get disrespectful, so get yo' girl and let her know what the fuck goin' on, man." I gave Dinero a look that let him know we'd be in that bitch tearing it up if she didn't take her ass on somewhere. I already knew how he was and as soon as I turned up on her he'd be ready to fight, and tonight I was with all the bullshit.

"Get me—"

"Bae, come here, man." He pulled her away, and I breathed

a sigh of relief as my pops came over with my mama right on his heels. They were clearly expecting answers and aside from Kash being gone and Camille being hurt in the process, I didn't have shit to tell them.

My mama immediately burst into tears, and he put his arm around her, looking just as fucked up as me. He was having to worry about his own mama and his grandson at the same time. We weren't used to shit like this, and the fact that we couldn't do shit but wait was eating away at us.

"Uhhh, family of Dorothea Harris!" As soon as we heard my granny's name, we all surrounded the doctor who looked stale in the face, and it instantly pissed me off. He didn't seem moved one way or another, so I couldn't even tell if I should've been hopeful or not.

"That's us. How's my mama doin'?" The pain was evident in my pops's voice, but that did little to change dude's crusty ass demeanor. Nodding, he looked over all of us with his beady blue eyes and then ducked his head into the clipboard he was holding.

"Okay, well, Ms. Harris suffered a severe myocardial infarction and—"

"Hold up, nigga, what? Use English, my guy!" I instantly cut in with my face balled up.

"It's um, it's a heart attack," he stammered, looking around at us like we were slow. I resisted the urge to hem his stupid ass up as he continued talking. "We were able to get her heart restarted, but the time without oxygen to the brain does take a toll on the body. She's stable, but she is comatose and hooked up to life support."

Anything else that nigga said faded out, and all I could see was red. My granny on life support, my girl being hurt, and my son being in the wind all were enough to turn me into a whole demon. Niggas definitely weren't ready for the type of havoc I was about to cause.....

To be continued

ALSO BY J. DOMINIQUE

Made in the USA
Columbia, SC
04 September 2024

41624382R00093